"*I knew it was a mistake taking her on here, Nicholas.*"

Lady Jessica's voice was filled with malevolence as she continued. "In fact, it was a huge mistake bringing her down to London in the first place."

Leigh's body was shaking with anger, but her feet remained glued to the spot.

"She's a cheap gold digger—we both know that." Lady Jessica went on. "And worse, she's going to try and get her claws into you."

There was deep laughter, then Lady Jessica's voice returned with increased anger. "You might laugh, but..." Her voice lowered, and Leigh turned away quickly, feeling sick.

CATHY WILLIAMS is Trinidadian and was brought up on the twin islands of Trinidad and Tobago. She was awarded a scholarship to study in Britain, and came to Exeter University in 1975 to continue her studies into the great loves of her life: languages and literature. It was there that Cathy met her husband, Richard. Since they married, Cathy has lived in England, originally in the Thames Valley but now in the Midlands. Cathy and Richard have three small daughters.

Books by Cathy Williams

HARLEQUIN PRESENTS
1413—A POWERFUL ATTRACTION
1502—CARIBBEAN DESIRE
1829—BEYOND ALL REASON
1909—ACCIDENTAL MISTRESS

CATHY WILLIAMS

Naïve Awakening

Harlequin Books

TORONTO • NEW YORK • LONDON
AMSTERDAM • PARIS • SYDNEY • HAMBURG
STOCKHOLM • ATHENS • TOKYO • MILAN
MADRID • WARSAW • BUDAPEST • AUCKLAND

ISBN 0-373-18674-6

NAÏVE AWAKENING

First North American Publication 1998.

CHAPTER ONE

ALL the anger was returning. It had been simmering away for the past two months, but now, here, outside the court, it erupted once again and Leigh felt all that rage rush to her head, making her momentarily giddy.

She squinted against the sun, the first they had had in that part of Yorkshire since summertime was officially declared four weeks ago, and sprinted the last few yards up to the stone stairs outside the local magistrates' court.

She had a very nice, biting little speech rehearsed in her head, which she was going to give her brother Freddie as soon as this dreadful affair was over and she had him to herself, on a one-to-one basis, and preferably somewhere enclosed so that all escape outlets were barred.

No, she would not be letting him get away with this, not in a hurry, maybe not ever. She had every intention of throwing it in his face every single time he so much as had a wayward thought. If he thought time had mellowed her attitude, then he was in for a shock.

Inside the stone building was chilly after the warmth outside, and she looked around dubiously, not quite sure where to go. Out of the corner of her eye she could see two officials looking at her, probably, she thought sourly, assuming that she was a criminal of some kind. After all, weren't criminals the only ones who set foot into places like these? The groups of people around her, standing about or walking towards one of the doors, looked normal enough, but who knew what they were there for? It could be anything.

She was sorely tempted to turn around and walk right back outside, but Freddie was expecting her, and besides it would be a waste of a perfectly good rehearsed speech, because she knew that if she did not do it while she was in this sort of mood, then she probably never would.

She adored her unruly little brother, the only person she had left in the world since their grandfather had died over eight months ago, and experience had taught her that he could charm her out of her most ferocious tempers. He would stare at her with those huge blue eyes, and she would feel her anger fizzling away.

But, she thought with a worried frown, boyish scrapes were quite a different matter from trouble with the law.

This time he had gone too far. He and those undisciplined so-called friends of his with whom he had taken up after their grandfather died. Stealing a car for a joyride was no laughing matter, even though he had only been a passenger in the back seat.

Worse, Sir John Reynolds, a man who had been one of her grandfather's closest friends, had been contacted by their local solicitor, and had seen fit to send his grandson to defend Freddie, to make sure that his copybook was not too blemished by this one-off incident.

The humiliation of it all.

She was so engrossed in her thoughts, walking quickly, head bent, in what she assumed was the right direction, that she almost ran straight into her brother.

There was a tall, dark-haired man at his side, but Leigh didn't see him at all. She focused all her attention on Freddie, who was beginning to look distinctly wary.

'Hi, sis,' he said cautiously.

Leigh stood completely still, her hands planted on her hips, her lips drawn into a narrow, angry line.

'Well?' she asked, fighting to be as firm and as unforgiving as she could. 'What was the outcome?' She still had not looked in the direction of the man who was standing a few feet away from her brother.

'Nicholas—Mr Reynolds—managed to persuade the judge hearing the case that it was all a horrible error of judgement. I was reprimanded, but that was all.' He attempted a reassuring smile which met with no change whatsoever in Leigh's expression.

She opened her mouth to begin her well-rehearsed lecture, when the man, whose presence she had ignored so far, spoke.

He had a deep voice. The sort of voice that people listened to.

'Well, well, well,' he was saying now, in a tone of voice which was infinitely mocking, 'little Leigh Taylor. I wondered what you would look like after all these years.'

They both turned towards him, Freddie with relief that the heat had been taken away from him, if only temporarily, and Leigh with outrage, as much by the fact that he had thrown her off course as by his tone of voice.

She raised her eyes to his face. Her memories of Nicholas Reynolds had been vague. They had grown up together for a while, been to the same school, albeit in wildly different forms because he was—she tried to think back—at least seven years older than she was. They had even played together, more through necessity than choice. His grandfather had spent a lot of time with hers, before the entire family had moved away from Yorkshire to London to live.

To say that he had grown up would, Leigh now felt, be somehow a huge understatement.

It would not begin to cover how vastly he had changed from the slightly aloof dark-haired little boy. For a start, there was nothing at all boyish about the man standing in front of her at all.

He was tall, powerfully built, with the same dark hair, but straighter now, and flint-grey eyes. The strong fea-

tures were etched into an expression of polite curiosity
as he looked at her.

As if, she thought, flushing, he were inspecting a
mildly interesting form of bacteria. True, she had not
changed much from her girlhood, still the same copper-
coloured hair, the same wide blue eyes, the same
stubborn, full mouth. Even so, it made her hackles rise
to see that he was staring at her as though she had not
changed at all, as though she were still the little girl he
used to tease all those years ago.

'Thank you for defending my brother, Mr Reynolds,'
she offered in a stilted voice. 'I can't imagine why our
solicitor contacted your grandfather. You needn't have
come this long way for something as trifling as a joyride
in a stolen car.'

'My grandfather,' he said, and it flashed through
Leigh's head that most barristers would give their eye-
teeth to sound like him, 'was very fond of Jacob. When
Jacob died, he told your solicitor to get in touch with
him if there was ever anything he could do for you and
your brother.'

'I see,' she replied, only in fact seeing that it seemed
a complete waste of Nicholas Reynolds's time. She knew,
from her grandfather's occasional comments over the
years, that he had excelled in law, and was constantly
in demand.

The feeling of humiliation washed over her again. He
must think them a couple of country bumpkins, she
thought, charity cases. And it was all Freddie's fault.

'Anyway,' she said awkwardly, her neck beginning to
ache from craning upwards to look at him, 'thanks for
your help and your time. When are you heading back
up to London?'

She knew that she should offer to take him out for a
meal, or something, but for some reason she shied away
from the invitation. Nicholas Reynolds made her feel

uncomfortable. He had always made her feel uncomfortable. Anyway, she just wanted to get that brother of hers back to their small house where she could corner him.

She would somehow have to drill it into his head that this brush with the law would be the first and only one, that she was deeply worried by her private thoughts that trifling matters such as those often led to more serious offences. She had a lot on her mind, and none of it involved the unwanted arrival of this city barrister with his aristocratic good looks and persuasive voice.

She refocused her attention on to Freddie, only to find herself again cut off before she could utter a word.

'Shall we discuss all this over coffee?' Nicholas said, in a voice that implied she had no choice in the matter, his hand on her elbow as he guided her towards the double doors.

Leigh felt his fingers on her bare flesh with a disconcerting prickle of heat, and drew her arm away.

'I'd love to,' she lied effusively, 'but I want to get Freddie back home.'

'Why?'

The question threw her because she had expected him to nod, say goodbye and leave the way he came. He was altogether too self-assured, too sophisticated, and too damned good-looking for her liking. Also the way he had stared at her when he'd first spoken to her, and said that he had wondered how she had turned out, still rankled. The lazy drawl had, for no reason at all, made her feel defensive, made her feel, for heaven's sake, like the gauche schoolgirl she had been all those years ago.

'Because,' she said patiently, 'we have a few things to discuss. Or rather I have a few things to say to him.' She shot Freddie a look that spoke volumes. 'Besides, I wouldn't want to detain you. I know that you've got better things to do with your time.'

'On the contrary. I haven't been back up this way for years. In fact, since the family left. It would be interesting to see how things have changed. And apart from that there are one or two things we need to talk about.' Again that hard, inflexible tone that made her uneasy. What was there to discuss?

He pushed open the door, and stood back, allowing her to walk past him, which she did, very quickly.

She didn't want him to think that she was nervous of him, but she was. Life in the fast lane had given him a cool edge of *savoir faire* which she was finding disconcerting.

She was not accustomed to men like him. She had grown up in a village where the people were simple, but friendly. They spoke their minds, and you always knew where you were with them.

Leigh had a feeling that Nicholas was the sort of man who only spoke his mind if it suited him. There was something watchful about him, watchful and controlled.

Next to her Freddie began babbling about inviting Nicholas back to the house, and Leigh turned to him and said sharply, 'Shut up.' She knew exactly why her younger brother was so keen on showing this virtual stranger all the delights of their little village. It was called buying time, and she was having none of it.

'I think your brother's right,' Nicholas said smoothly. He smiled at her, a charming smile that could not quite hide the fact that he somehow disapproved of the situation in which he had found himself, and Leigh frowned.

'Well, we could head back to the village and have coffee there,' she said grudgingly, hearing her brother expel a long sigh of relief. 'Did you drive up here?'

Nicholas nodded. 'I'll follow you, shall I? My car's just there.' He indicated a sleek Jaguar parked across the road, and Leigh thought that it was just the sort of car she would have expected him to drive.

'I'll go with Nicholas,' Freddie piped up, 'to show him the way.'

'Don't think I don't know what game you're playing,' she whispered fiercely under her breath. In a louder voice, she said, 'Fine.'

Nicholas was looking at them both closely. We're a species apart as far as he's concerned, Leigh thought acidly. She looked at him again. Under the merciless rays of the sun, he was even more commanding that he had appeared in the shadowy bowels of the court. His black hair was thick and springy, his eyes shrewd and observant. He was staring back at her, and Leigh refused to be deflated. He was in her part of the world now, and as far as she was concerned she would look at him for just as long as she wanted.

Her eyes travelled the length of him, taking in the lovingly tailored cut of his suit, the likes of which she had never seen before apart from on television, the broad muscularity of his chest, the long, clever fingers, the patent leather shoes.

An expensive city animal, she thought wryly, a predator in the concrete jungle. It was unbelievable that he had ever spent any time at all living in Yorkshire, where the people could be as harsh as the weather.

'Do you normally subject the men you meet to such careful appraisals?' he asked.

'Men like you don't normally frequent this part of the world,' she said evenly. 'You're a rarity here. Just as we're a rarity for you. I'm merely subjecting you, as you call it, to the same sort of observation.'

'*Touché.*'

'Shall we go, then?' Freddie asked, grinning at his sister's ill humour.

He had stuffed his hands into the pockets of the suit which she had made him buy for the hearing, and in which he looked decidedly uncomfortable, and was hovering in a manner that suggested he had much better things to do than stand around in the baking sun.

What options did she have? Precisely none. Her well-rehearsed speech had flown right out of her head, and she spent the short journey back to the village fuming.

Ever so often she glanced into the rear-view mirror, and the sight of Nicholas behind the steering-wheel made her feel even angrier.

By the time they made it to the village and had parked their cars she had made up her mind to make any social patter over coffee as brief as she possibly could, and if he didn't like her attitude then he could lump it.

Freddie was looking decidedly more relaxed. He shot her a wheedling smile, and asked whether he could go home.

Leigh looked at him, irritated to find that she was suddenly appalled at the prospect of being alone with Nicholas Reynolds.

'Why do you want to go home?' she prevaricated.

'I have some study to catch up on.'

There was no answer to that one. It was rare enough that Freddie volunteered to study, usually relying on the fact that he was innately bright to get him through exams.

He grinned coyly at Leigh, as though fully aware that he had trapped her into submission.

'Fine. You can also clean the house,' she informed him, refusing to be beaten by a cheeky sixteen-year-old, 'fix the kitchen door and take the dustbins out.'

'Why do I have to fix the kitchen door? It works all right to me.'

'It's falling off its hinges.'

'It doesn't matter; I mean, there's just the two of us, and——'

'Just fix it, Freddie, or else you can stay put and ac-company us to the coffee-shop, and afterwards you can come with me to the shoe shop so that I can get you some new shoes, and then to the barber for a haircut.'

She knew that the new shoes and the haircut would swing the argument in her favour, and it did. Freddie hurried off, promising to fix the kitchen door first thing, after awkwardly thanking Nicholas once again for getting him out of a jam.

'Jam indeed. I'll soon straighten him on that score,' Leigh muttered under her breath. She looked at Nicholas, resisted looking at her watch, and said, 'Shall we go?' And get this over with, her tone implied.

'There's no rush, you know,' he said softly, as though reading her mind, but he fell in step with her, and as it turned out she was the one who had to hurry, merely to keep pace with him.

They walked through the village, with Nicholas commenting politely on how little had changed since he was last there.

'Nothing needs to change,' Leigh said curtly, 'we're perfectly happy with the way things are. We don't need tall buildings and fast cars, and all the glamorous trappings that go with big city life. We don't need to barricade ourselves into our houses because we're scared of people breaking in. We all know each other here...'

'And that's the way we like it,' Nicholas finished for her.

Leigh glanced sharply at him. Was he mocking her or was she just imagining it? His tone of voice had been pleasant enough, but there was something about it that she found disturbing.

Was he implying that she was somehow insular? Not for the first time, she wondered what her life would have been if she had left Yorkshire and gone to one of the bigger cities to live. Leeds, perhaps, even maybe London.

The situation had never arisen, and she had never really engineered it, being perfectly happy to have the rugged, beautiful Yorkshire dales all around her, even though she had sacrificed the opportunity to study art at college. She had settled instead for a safe job at the local library, which she rather enjoyed, and looking after her grandfather, which she had enjoyed rather more.

He had raised them ever since her parents had died in a plane crash when she was a child, and she had never once begrudged taking over the job of caring for him as he became older.

Now this suave outsider, because he was an outsider even though he had spent part of his life here, was beginning to addle her, beginning to make her think of things beyond the Yorkshire boundaries. Made her feel hot and defensive, although she couldn't quite put a finger on why he should be able to do so.

He was remarking on shops which were still around from his boyhood days, and she said sweetly, 'You wouldn't be so amazed at all this if you had made an effort to come back here now and again.'

Nicholas turned to face her. 'Outspoken, aren't you?'

'We all are in this part of the world.'

As though to prove her point, Mrs Evans, the middle-aged lady who ran the post office with her husband, came up to them, and greeted her.

'Aren't you going to introduce us, lass?' she asked, looking at Nicholas with interest.

'Nicholas Reynolds,' Leigh said reluctantly. 'He came here to help with Freddie.'

'Oh, yes. He was a bit off the rails, your Freddie, wasn't he? Jacob would be turning in his grave. Nicholas Reynolds—Reynolds, name rings a bell...'

Nicholas gave her one of his charming smiles.

Leigh, looking at him, was suddenly struck by his attractiveness, his masculinity. He was, she thought with shock, more than simply attractive, he was sexy. What must he think of her? Of course, she couldn't care less, but even so she must appear a complete peasant to him.

She had dressed informally because of the weather, and was wearing only a summery cotton skirt in shades of blue and purple, and a short-sleeved jersey with buttons down the front. She wore no make-up, and had plaited her waist-length hair into a French braid which hung down her back.

No wonder he had looked disapprovingly at her as though she were a schoolgirl, barely older than sixteen-year-old Freddie, instead of the twenty-three-year-old woman that she was.

He was probably accustomed to a quite different type of woman. Even looking at him, any fool would know that he moved in that rarified world of the wealthy and powerful. The women who inhabited that world were no doubt as sophisticated and urbane as he was, leggy blondes with impeccably made-up faces and smiles that never quite reached their eyes.

Leigh pursed her lips defensively, determined not to try and pretend to be anything other than what she was.

He was chatting amiably to Mrs Evans, and the older woman was responding to his charm with blushing smiles and coy motions of protestation when he told her that he remembered her well from his youth, and that she hadn't aged a bit.

'Isn't he terrible?' she said, turning to Leigh. 'Hasn't he grown up into a fine-looking young man, and such a charmer!'

Leigh hoped that Mrs Evans was not expecting any sort of response to her observations, but just in case she was she said succinctly, 'He seems pretty much the same to me. Just older. As for his charm, I'm immune to it. I remember too clearly when he used to tease me.'

'I don't remember teasing you,' Nicholas murmured to her, after Mrs Evans had left.

'You used to derive a great deal of pleasure from pulling my hair.'

'Well, it doesn't seem to have done it any harm. It's still as long and silky as I remember.'

Leigh blushed bright red and told herself to get her act together. He might have some kind of charm, but he could forget it if he thought that he could use it on her. She might be a country girl, but that didn't mean that she was a gullible idiot.

She led him towards the coffee-shop, waiting impatiently while Mr Baird, who owned it, accosted her in a very similar manner to Mrs Evans. He too regarded Nicholas with undisguised interest, and Leigh fervently hoped that the scrutiny went some way to making him feel out of place. Though, she thought, eyeing him from under her lashes, it didn't seem to. He seemed as at home with these rugged, kindly people as she herself was.

She childishly thought it wasn't fair.

'I'm glad we're here alone,' he said, as they waited for their coffee and cakes. Mr Baird's wife baked all the cakes herself and Leigh could never resist the opportunity of having one. 'There's something I want to talk to you about, and it'll be easier without Freddie around.' Something in his voice made her look at him warily.

'If you're going to lecture me about Freddie's brush with the law,' she began haughtily, 'then you might as well forget it. I'm fully aware that what he did was wrong, and, believe it or not, so is he. He's never done anything like this before, and he won't again. He's just gone off the rails a bit since Grandad died. They were very close. You don't have to tell me that I'm going to need to take a firm hand with him, because that's exactly what I intend to do. In fact, I'd be doing it now if I weren't here instead, taking a trip with you down memory lane.'

So there, she implied.

Nicholas leaned back in the small chair, his broad frame looking absurdly out of place on the fragile wooden structure, and watched her impassively.

'Quite a speech,' he drawled with infuriating calm, not in the least put out by her insinuation that he was somehow wasting her time, 'but as a barrister I've seen all too well how young boys like Freddie can wind up in gaol, and, believe me, speeches and good intentions can get lost in the wind very easily.'

He looked at her thoughtfully, and when he spoke his voice was polite but hard. 'I fully appreciate that it must be difficult for you—you're scarcely out of childhood yourself—but don't lull yourself into believing that things like this can get swept under the carpet after a strong talking-to.'

Leigh looked at him speechlessly. How dared he waltz into their lives and start preaching to her about Freddie's upbringing?

'Are you suggesting that I'm not competent enough to look after my brother?'

'Did I say that?'

'Please don't play these verbal games with me,' she said, making an effort to modulate her voice.

'All right,' he replied smoothly, 'then let me ask you this; what do you intend to do with him now?'

Leigh frowned and had an uneasy feeling that she was being ushered into a trap. 'I have no idea what you mean,' she said at last. 'I intend to give him a sound ticking off, and keep my eye on him to make sure that he doesn't get into any more trouble. Although, as I said, I think he's learnt a lesson from this. Freddie's no fool. I can't see him doing this sort of thing again in a hurry. He'll listen to me. He won't end up in gaol!'

'You mean, that's what you hope. Tell me something; did you have any idea that he would be involved in this sort of incident?'

'Well, I know that he hadn't exactly been disciplined since Grandad died, but——'

'And you really think that you can remedy that problem?'

'Yes, I do!' Her cheeks were flaming, and she stood up, quite prepared to walk out of the shop and to hell with any need to be grateful and polite.

'Sit back down,' he grated, and his words held enough of a command in them for her to reluctantly obey.

'You can't tell me how to run my life,' she muttered mutinously.

'I don't need to,' he said smoothly. 'The mere fact that I'm here says it all, don't you agree?'

There was very little that she could say to that, but the sheer logic of what he had just said didn't stop her from feeling furiously angry. Angry at his arrogance, at his assumption that he could write off all her efforts with her brother without so much as an apology, and particularly angry at the way that he had somehow found precisely the right crack in her armour to render her defenceless.

Ever since Freddie's arrest she had been plagued by self-doubts and by her anxiety at realising that her attempts to stabilise him after their grandfather's death had clearly failed.

But the last thing she needed was Nicholas Reynolds reminding her of the fact in that patronising tone of voice.

'Well, then,' she said frozenly, 'what do you suggest I do? Keep him chained to his bed as a lesson in discipline?'

'I suggest,' he said in measured tones, 'that you leave Yorkshire.'

Mr Baird had brought them a plateful of home-made cakes, and she bit into one, eyeing him defensively over the pink icing.

'What?' she asked, not sure that she had heard correctly.

'Leave Yorkshire.'

'What a good idea,' she bit out sarcastically, 'perhaps we could rob a bank and spend the proceeds recuperating on the French Riviera. I hate to sound rude, Mr Reynolds——'

'Nicholas, please. After all, it's not as though we don't know each other.'

She ignored his interruption. 'But I resent you swanning up here with a bag full of good intentions and telling me how to run my life here. I have a good job at the library, and Freddie will settle down.'

'And what if he doesn't?'

Leigh almost choked on a mouthful of coffee. Just who did this man think he was anyway? Was he daring to tell her how to run her life? What right did he think he had?

Freddie was her responsibility, and she wasn't going to have anyone preaching to her on her suitability as his guardian.

He clicked his tongue impatiently. 'For God's sake, stop acting as though I'm the big, bad wolf who has nothing better to do than pick on you.'

Leigh's blue eyes stormily met his cool grey ones. She didn't care for this man one jot, even as a boy he had managed to get under her skin, so why was she even listening to him as though she were being cross-examined in a witness box instead of sitting in Mr Baird's coffee-shop?

'What,' he continued implacably, 'do you, for instance, intend to do about Freddie's education?'

'He's just sat his exams, and he'll be leaving school...'

'And do you think that's fair? He's a bright boy; what will he be leaving school to do? He told me that he would

like to go on to specialise in cabinet-making, but that
he didn't know whether he would be able to or not.'

'He told you that?'

'Yes,' Nicholas informed her.

Leigh surveyed him in silence. Right at this instant,
it was a good thing that Freddie wasn't around, because
she could quite happily have strangled him.

She knew what he wanted well enough, but money
was tight, and she had guiltily thought that he had accepted the fact. She had discussed it with him, and told
him that he could do whatever he wanted after he had
worked for a while and got some money together. It was
the only thing she could think of.

How could he just go and pour out all their personal
problems to a stranger?

God knew what else he had told this aggravating Mr
Know-it-all.

'There's not much chance of that, not just at the
moment. Maybe some time in the future.'

'Because of your financial situation.'

Leigh nodded reluctantly. 'Grandad's money will really
only help to keep the cottage running. It needs some
pretty expensive repairs which we had all been putting
off for a while, and which can't be postponed for much
longer. The roof needs work doing on it, I really would
like to get some central heating put in, it needs re-
painting on the outside...' Her voice trailed off.

'The list goes on.'

'More or less,' she shrugged, hating the admission and
thinking of all the other million and one things that still
needed doing around the place, 'but we can manage.
With my salary, we should be able to muddle along.'

'And what about you? Are you going to be happy just
muddling along?'

There it was: that underlying criticism that made her
feel somehow inadequate. If that was all he had to say,

then she sincerely wished that he would just shut up. Did he really think she was depriving her brother of what he wanted through some perverted sense of enjoyment?

'I don't see where all this is leading, Mr Reynolds. Oh, sorry,' she said with honeyed insincerity, 'Nicholas. I can't change the way things are at the moment, so if I have to accept us just muddling along for the time being, then I will.'

'Have you thought about trying to change things?'

'Have you thought about not sticking your nose into other people's business?'

She felt a heel as soon as the words were out of her mouth, but she couldn't take them back, so she looked down at her empty coffee-cup, refusing to meet his eyes.

'I'll choose to ignore that statement, though I'd like to remind you that I'm only here at all at my grand-father's request,' he said with silky smoothness, and she didn't answer. She had known from the very first moment that she had set eyes on Nicholas Reynolds that he was a force to be reckoned with, but she had not known to what extent.

He was forcing her to face a few things which she would have been much happier ignoring for the time being, and she didn't care for it one little bit.

The fact that he was worlds apart from her only served to make things worse.

She glared at him, very tempted to tell him that he could choose to ignore it or not, it really didn't matter to her. Instead she said in as controlled a voice as she could muster, 'What do you suggest? I can't change the way things are, I just have to cope the best that I can.'

She glared at him, highly annoyed that he had managed to nettle her when she should just have ignored everything he had to say. True, she was outspoken, but that was simply the way of the world around here. She was not normally given to shouting matches, and she found it infuriating that he was bringing out this side of her.

From behind the counter Mr Baird was looking in her direction with open curiosity. Now, she thought, it would be all around the village that she had had an argument with the lawyer from London, and what on earth could it be about?

She forced herself to smile at Nicholas.

'When will you be heading back? You never said.'

It was an obvious switch in the conversation, and one which he ignored totally.

'I've spoken with your solicitor about your financial state of affairs, and you're finding it difficult to make ends meet, aren't you? Admit it, that cottage of yours is falling down around your ears, isn't it?'

'That's privileged information,' Leigh gasped, horrified.

'I persuaded your solicitor that it was in your interests not to keep me in the dark about your state of affairs.'

'How thoughtful of you. So now that you've discovered what a wicked guardian I am, and how desperately badly off we are, you can climb into that expensive car of yours and clear off back to London. I'm of course very grateful for everything you've done, for putting yourself out, but, before you tell me yet again that we both need a change of scenery, we can't afford it. As you have already found out for yourself.'

She had the awful feeling that everything private in her had just been scooped out and held up for public ridicule. Now all she wanted was to go back to the cottage and put any memories of this man to the very back of her mind.

'Not so simple, I hate to disappoint you.' He signalled to Mr Baird to bring them a fresh pot of coffee, and asked her whether she wanted any more cake.

She had already eaten three, but she nodded and asked Mr Baird if he could bring her one of his wife's special custard-filled eclairs. She felt as though she needed it.

'Are you normally such a voracious eater?' he asked curiously. 'No, don't tell me, it's the fresh country air. Unlike all that dirty smog you get in London, which has everyone turning away from food and walking around with sallow, pale complexions.'

Another injection of comic relief, she thought sourly. At my expense.

'Hilarious,' Leigh said.

'Anyway, where was I? Oh, yes, I can't leave just yet, because you're quite wrong. I didn't only drive here so that I could help your brother.'

'Really.' She watched him with a nervous sensation in the pit of her stomach and wondered where all this was leading.

'No. You see, my grandfather was horrified when he learnt about Freddie's trouble. He and your grandfather, as you know, were very close. In fact, my grandfather considered Jacob one of his few true friends, someone who liked him for reasons that had nothing whatsoever to do with his title, or his money. He often said that Jacob was the only man who never hesitated to give him a lecture if he thought that it was necessary.'

Leigh felt a lump come to her throat at Nicholas's words. She knew exactly what he meant. Her grandfather had been a down-to-earth, totally frank, and very caring man. He would never have been impressed by all the superficial paraphernalia which most people judged each other by.

'Anyway,' Nicholas continued, 'when my grandfather heard about Freddie, he proposed that not only should I come up here, but that I should bring you both back to London with me so that he could look after both of you.'

'What?'

'You heard.'

'I might have heard,' Leigh said tersely, 'but I didn't believe. Look, I know your grandfather means well, and tell him thanks, but no, thanks. We can manage just fine here on our own. We don't need charity.'

'There's no question of charity,' Nicholas said in a cool voice. 'My grandfather suggested it because it's what he wants to do. As for not needing it, from the looks of it, you most certainly do.'

'What do you mean?' Leigh abandoned all attempt to be polite.

'I think it would do you both good to leave Yorkshire for a while. My grandfather would pay for Freddie to go to college to study carpentry, which is what he wants to do, isn't it?'

'I can't just pack in my job and go to London. What about Grandad's cottage? Who's going to look after it?'

'A caretaker.'

'I can't accept your grandfather's offer.'

'You would sacrifice your brother's ambitions because of pride?'

'It's not as simple as that,' she muttered helplessly. 'I have a job here. I'd never be able to pay you back, and I won't be indebted.'

'Oh, you won't have to be.' He leaned back in the chair and looked at her unhurriedly through narrowed eyes. 'Believe me, my grandfather may be overflowing with the milk of human kindness for you and your brother, but the sentiment isn't shared. Oh, no, you won't be coming to London to enjoy a free ride with us. You can work for me, and as far as I can see that would sort out both our problems.'

CHAPTER TWO

IT WAS ten days before Leigh and Freddie found themselves at King's Cross station in London.

She had managed to persuade old Mr Edwards, one of her grandfather's friends, to keep a regular eye on the cottage for them, in return for which she would keep him supplied in cherry pies whenever she made them. It had seemed a fair deal. In fact, it was only deal available since her finances couldn't quite stretch to hiring a full-time caretaker.

Nicholas had been spot on target when he had pointed out her cash flow problems to her. The fact was that her money—what little she earned from her job and the small amount left to her by her grandfather—was just enough to make ends meet, and that was with some very acrobatic economising.

Which, she had thought bleakly after he had left, had been the crux of the problem. And he had manipulated it like the persuasive, successful barrister that he was.

Hadn't he known instinctively what argument to use on her? That it was for Freddie's benefit? And she, who had never been persuaded to do anything which she did not want to do, had found herself put into a position in which she could barely manoeuvre. She must go to London for the sake of her brother's future and her own finances and stomach the fact that she was in a trap.

It had only been her brother's enthusiasm for the idea that had stopped her from calling him up and telling him where he could put his stupid suggestion.

As for the job he had thrown her, she was sharp enough to realise that it was a gesture only partly designed to ease her conscience. After all, she thought, surveying the nerve-racking impersonality of the platform crowds, what did he care about her conscience? No, having mulled it all over, she could see quite clearly that his offer of a job was far more designed to ensure that he wasn't lumbered with a couple of unwelcome unpaying guests. He basically didn't want them cluttering up his smart London life, but since he had had little choice in the matter, what better than to make sure that she work for her keep?

She wondered whether he thought that they would stick to his grandfather's generosity like two parasites and shamelessly eat them out of house and home.

Oh, he had exploited the situation admirably, and as far as she was concerned had left her bereft of any pride.

Now here they were, standing on the platform of a station the size of which she had never seen before, surrounded by their clutter of battered suitcases, some of which had been tied with string, and no porter in sight.

What seemed like thousands of people, more people in fact than lived in her entire village, hurried around them, carefully side-stepping their bags, intent on their business. In Yorkshire, she thought ruefully, there would have been no shortage of people willing to help them.

Her brother was lost in the novelty of it all, as he had been from the very minute he had stepped on to the train at their tiny station.

Leigh looked at him affectionately and promptly ordered him to go and find a trolley.

'Where?' he asked.

'I don't know,' she said irritably, 'just go and get one. If we wait for someone to come along and help us, we'll be here till we go grey.'

He ambled off obediently, and left her to her thoughts. More doubts and a feeling of being completely out of her depth. She had been to Leeds a few times before, but only once to London when she was very young, when Freddie was only a baby, and it was as vast and confusing as she remembered.

She only hoped that Nicholas was outside waiting for them, as he had promised he would be, because if he wasn't it would be another nightmare of waiting for a taxi to take them to the house in Hampstead.

Oh, God, she thought, why on earth had she ever agreed to come here? She didn't belong here, she belonged in the country, where people only dressed up for special occasions, and the busiest place was the local market.

Here, everyone seemed so smartly dressed, lots of high heels and tailored skirts everywhere, and the men walking briskly in their suits and carrying briefcases! She couldn't remember her grandfather ever wearing a suit, although he must have possessed one at some point in time.

She glanced down at her own outfit, a light flowered sleeveless dress falling softly around her slim figure, and a pair of sandals. She had even brought her straw hat with her, to protect her face from the sun.

She was quite pale-skinned, with a smattering of freckles, which always came out with a vengeance if she wasn't very careful in the sun. She wished now that she had forgotten about the hat, because she imagined that it only served to emphasise how rustic she was.

Freddie returned with a trolley, and after what seemed like ages they managed to find their way through the ticket barrier, and outside the station, which was every bit as crowded as it had been outside.

'Wow,' Freddie crowed, staring around him, 'have you ever seen crowds like these?'

'Ask me whether I ever wanted to.'

'Stop being so miserable,' Freddie said, turning to her with a frown.

'I'm not being miserable. I just miss all the open space.'

'I don't.'

'I know you don't. You're like a little boy at Christmas-time!'

They laughed and she put her arm around him, noticing with amusement how he edged out of her embrace. Sisterly cuddles were taboo with him, especially sisterly cuddles administered in public.

She was looking around for Nicholas, when she heard his deep voice from behind her.

'So I see you managed to find your way here all right.'

She swung around, blushing as the grey eyes ran over her, feeling oddly as though his scrutiny was stripping her of her clothing.

'Yes. No problem at all.' She was here now, and she would be polite, but there was no reason why she should be friendly. She couldn't forget those thinly veiled insinuations that she was irresponsible when it came to Freddie, and a potential gold-digger who would be given a job if the alternative was her sponging off their hospitality.

'Good.' He picked up the cases as though they weighed nothing at all and began striding away. Leigh hurried behind him, clutching her hat, oddly mesmerised by his easy, graceful walk. There was nothing clumsy or cumbersome about him. In fact, from behind, he could well pass for an athlete of some kind.

He was chatting to Freddie, answering all his excited questions, getting along with him as though they had known each other for years. Obviously his hostility did not extend to her brother.

She would, she thought, have to have a serious word with him about being careful not to let London go to his head, and to remember that he was a country lad at heart. The last thing she wanted was for him to change.

The gleaming Jaguar seemed to fill Freddie with as much reverential awe as it had the last time he had seen it.

'It's just a car, Freddie,' Leigh commented, halting his monologue on its engine capacity in mid-flow, and missing Nicholas's raised eyebrow. 'Metal on four wheels, designed to get you from A to B.' She slid into the front seat and strapped herself in, inwardly admiring the walnut dashboard and the deep, luxurious seats.

'A lot of women would be very impressed by this particular piece of metal on four wheels,' Nicholas murmured, as he started the engine. His eyes slid along to her face, and Leigh purposefully ignored both him and the little leap of her pulse.

'Really?' she said, gazing with mixed feelings through the window. 'I can't see why. As far as I'm concerned, the last thing that would impress me about a man would be his car. Or, for that matter, the sort of house he lived in, or the kind of clothes he wore. All that's superficial and doesn't say a thing about the kind of person he is.' So, she wanted to add, you needn't worry that I'm after your money.

'And have you been impressed by any men?'

Leigh frowned and didn't answer, because as far as she was concerned it was none of his business whatsoever.

'No,' Freddie chipped in from the back seat, 'she hasn't had a boyfriend for ages, since she broke up with Dean Stanley, in fact.'

'I'll thank you to not go broadcasting my private affairs to all and sundry,' she snapped. 'You're not too old to rediscover the meaning of punishment.'

Freddie made a face at her and resumed his attention to what they were passing, and Nicholas, she was annoyed to see, was looking vaguely amused by the interchange.

'Anyway,' she said in a honeyed voice, 'is that why you drive this? So that you can impress girls?'

'I don't go out with girls,' he replied, not at all disconcerted by her sarcasm, 'I go out with women. And I don't need to impress them with a car.'

Leigh refused to ask him what sort of things he used to impress them. There was an intonation to his voice, something soft and insinuating, that sent her mind racing and she firmly slapped it right back into place.

He took them a circuitous route, on Freddie's pleading, pointing out all the sights to them, and still with that very slight edge of amusement to his voice, which went completely over Freddie's head, but didn't go over hers one bit.

After a while, though, she found herself listening to what he was saying, and actually enjoying his amusing descriptions of the buildings and landmarks. He had a dry wit which made her chuckle on a couple of occasions, even though she reminded herself that she didn't care for him, or, for that matter, what he represented.

It was slightly over an hour later when the car pulled through the heavy gates which led on to the small courtyard in front of the house. The gardens were not massive—Leigh supposed that in London land was at a premium—but the house made up for that. It was enormous, the impressive frontage studded with numerous leaded windows.

Freddie whistled under his breath, and she said wryly, 'I can see that there won't be a shortage of space here. Do you realise that your house is bigger than the one hotel in our village?'

'I thought you weren't impressed by outward trappings.'

'I'm not,' she retorted, rising to his bait, 'I'm merely stating a fact. Do you and your grandfather live here alone?'

'Most of the year. My parents come over for two months every winter, and there are several people who help look after the house and garden.'

The Jaguar pulled up outside the front door, and Leigh stepped outside, her hat clutched firmly in both hands, her head thrown back as she studied the grandeur of the place. She had not bothered to tie her hair back and it fell down her back, silken copper set ablaze by the sun.

Nicholas had stopped a few feet behind her. He shook his head, as if clearing it of some niggling thought, and brushed past her, opening the front door which had been double locked.

At once there was an oldish man there, waiting to take their cases, and another middle-aged woman hovering in the background, waiting to show them to their respective bedrooms.

Leigh would have preferred to stay where she was for a while, and admire the house, if house was the right word. The décor was impeccable, all shades of white and cream, with just enough colour from the pictures on the walls and the huge pots of flowering plants to stop it from sliding into blandness.

A huge winding staircase, stripped with deep burgundy carpeting, ran to the upstairs bedrooms, and probably continued further. She knew, from the outside of the house, that there were three floors. Three floors of rooms all sumptuously decorated.

Freddie had snatched up his two cases and was taking the stairs two by two, overtaking the maid. He disappeared from sight, and Leigh turned to Nicholas, who had been observing her from a distance.

'I don't think I've managed,' she almost choked on the words, 'to thank you and of course your grandfather for kindly asking us here. Freddie's delighted at the prospect of going to college for his course.'

'And I gather from your tone of voice that you still haven't worked yourself up to sharing his enthusiasm?'

'No,' she replied stiffly, thinking that it was difficult to become excited over emotional blackmail.

'You could always have stayed in Yorkshire, you know, and made do with your rambling cottage which would have progressively eaten up more and more of your money, and your job at the library which just paid enough to keep the food on the table.'

'You might as well know, I wouldn't be here now if it weren't for Freddie.'

'But you are, aren't you?' he countered smoothly. The grey eyes swept over her with cool calculation. 'And you can stop acting as though you're the only one who's suffering a change of lifestyle. As I said, the only reason I bailed your brother out was because of my grandfather.'

'Are you trying to say that you don't want us around?'

'I'm trying to say that you've been rescued from a difficult situation, and . . .'

'I should be grateful,' she finished for him. She felt all her good intentions to be polite with this man draining away from her. Yet again.

'Shouldn't you?'

'Yes,' she said tightly. Grateful, she added silently, for being in a gilded cage, because she was caged— trapped by a situation over which all control had been removed from her.

'I don't expect gratitude, Leigh,' he said in a hard voice, 'but I do expect you to stop acting like a martyr all of the time. Now perhaps you'd like to go upstairs and freshen up?'

'Perhaps I would,' she agreed, stinging from his reprimand, but knowing that she had more less provoked him into it. 'Where is my room?'

'I'll show you up.' He started up the stairs, and Leigh followed him.

Everything about him, his movements, his speech, that watchful, cool air about him, spelt power and self-assurance, and just a hint of arrogance. He was so totally different from all those boys she had been out with in the past. So totally different from her, she conceded. She would do well to remember that.

He began talking to her about his grandfather, telling her how much he had changed after the death of his wife years ago. 'He hardly ever leaves the house,' Nicholas said. 'He says that he's simply counting down to the day when he'll no longer be around. He comes down for meals, and he uses the library on the ground floor a lot, and that's really about it.'

Leigh thought that it was a shame. Her own grandfather had been full of beans right up to the end. Even in those last few weeks, when his illness had made getting around difficult, he had still insisted on taking his walks, on keeping as active as he possibly could.

Her bedroom was on the top floor, along with Freddie's. Nicholas pushed open the door, and she stepped inside. Her bags had been brought up and were on the floor next to the gigantic old wardrobe. All the furniture in the bedroom, in fact, was old, from the dressing-table and chairs, to the bureau sitting next to the tall, leaded window, and, of course, the four-poster bed.

'It's wonderful,' she breathed, forgetting his presence temporarily and padding across the floor, her hands trailing along the furniture, her eyes taking in absolutely everything. A small en-suite bathroom had been added at some later stage, and had been fitted out in colours of apricot and green, with matching bath towels.

Nicholas had been lounging by the door, and now he walked into the room and looked around it briefly.

'It's home.' He shrugged and walked across to the window. 'I suppose I've become used to it.'

'I suppose you would,' Leigh said drily, 'although you wouldn't, if you had any inkling of the hardship that a lot of people have to endure. I know some people who have slaved all their lives, working the pits, or toiling in factories, and for all their hard work they will never be able to know what it is to have this sort of comfort. The problem with wealth is that it cushions you against all of life's unpleasantness, doesn't it?'

'Does it? Don't you think that that's a little bit of a generalisation? Why don't you stop dividing people into categories, and start realising that everyone has something to offer?'

'That's unfair! I don't divide people into categories.'

Nicholas moved to where she was, and before she could escape to some other, safer part of the room he was standing next to her, far too close for comfort.

'You,' he said, coiling his fingers into her long, unruly hair and tilting her head to face him, 'have got to be the most argumentative, stubborn woman I have ever met in my life. And I've met my fair share of women.'

Leigh stared at his dark, handsome face in silence. She wanted to fire back with a retort. In normal circumstances she could hold her own in any argument, was rarely at a loss for words, but somehow her mouth had managed to go dry and wouldn't do what she wanted it to.

She had a swift feeling of giddiness, and then she blinked and reality returned.

'Believe me, the last thing I'm interested in is the number of women in your life!'

Her heart was beating heavily, and she could feel her hands clammy and tightly clenched at her sides. She just wanted to get away from this man. He was overpowering her.

There was a knock on the door, and Freddie bounded in. Nicholas released her abruptly, and her moment of confusion and alarm was over.

She retreated to her suitcases, which she began dumping on the bed, and chatted to Freddie, her words spilling over each other as she tried to shove the effect that Nicholas had had on her to the back of her mind.

Freddie was in high spirits. He wanted to do everything, see everything, yesterday. He had already unpacked, which meant that he had thrown all his clothes into the nearest available drawers and cupboards, and was now raring to go. He somehow managed to persuade Nicholas to take him to Piccadilly Circus, which he had heard about, on the Underground of course, and Leigh couldn't resist a grin as she tried to picture Nicholas squashed in the middle of a crowded train.

'Nicholas probably has to return to work,' she said, trying to wipe the smile off her face.

This thought had obviously not crossed Freddie's mind. 'Oh,' he said, deflated, 'can't you take the day off?'

'Freddie!'

'It's all right, Freddie. I already have, and it's just as well that you become acquainted with London as soon as possible.'

Freddie bounded back out of the room, an excitable puppy whose energy left Leigh feeling exhausted, and Nicholas turned to her.

'I don't suppose you'll share the joke with me?'

'Joke? What joke?'

'The one you were grinning at a few minutes ago.'

Leigh blew a strand of her hair from her face, and said obligingly, 'I will, actually. I was trying to imagine you on the Underground, with elbows and newspapers sticking into you, like a sardine in a tin.'

'I see,' Nicholas said thoughtfully. 'Well, I find it equally hilarious to picture you on the Underground, sticky and uncomfortable and moaning about how much you'd wished you'd stayed in Yorkshire.'

'Just as well as I'm not coming with you, then, isn't it,' she replied tartly, 'so you'll have to forgo the opportunity to laugh at me?'

Once he was out of the room, she ran a hot bath and settled into the suds with delicious enjoyment.

Over the past fortnight, she had barely had time to think, and now, in the silence of the room, her mind played around all the quickfire sequence of events that had occurred recently. It was unbelievable. Plucked from her rural home town and catapulted into London, and not just London, but the London champagne set, because she knew without being told that that was where Nicholas belonged.

It was like Cinderella at the ball, she thought, but an unwilling Cinderella without the fancy dress. She was the plain-clothed, plain-speaking rustic in a world which no doubt operated on various levels of innuendo and subterfuge.

She had as yet met none of his friends, and it was an experience which she was not looking forward to.

She wondered whether they would all be like Nicholas. The men all tall, and debonair, and the women sophisticated and bursting with *savoir faire*.

It was hard to imagine anyone quite like him, but maybe that was simply because she had never moved in this sort of world.

A sudden thought struck her: had she brought the right sort of clothes? Flowered print dresses, sandals and jeans might be all right in her small home town, but would they look out of place here? She mentally shrugged and decided that people could take her as they found her; she certainly didn't intend losing much sleep over it.

Later on, when she was dressing for dinner, she looked dubiously at her wardrobe once again, finding it slightly more difficult this time to dismiss the thought that the things she had brought with her really were a bit on the well-worn side.

She had somehow not managed to do any shopping for the past few months, none at all in fact since the death of her grandfather, and a lot of her stuff seemed that touch faded. Of course, it didn't matter one jot, she told herself defiantly, choosing a green uncluttered dress to wear that evening. She was meeting Sir John and she wanted to look just right.

Nicholas was eating out, and wasn't going to be in until later, probably when they were having coffee.

Just as well, she thought, staring at her face in the mirror, wondering whether to put on any make-up and deciding against it. She was too sensitive to his presence to really relax with him.

Sir John was waiting for her in the sitting-room when she went down a few minutes later. Leigh introduced Freddie, and as the old man chatted to him she took the opportunity to observe him.

She barely remembered him. He couldn't have been much older than her grandfather, but he certainly looked it. There were lines of resignation and disappointment around his mouth and his eyes were faded and blue as though he had spent years looking at things that he found depressing.

He turned to her and began talking.

Even his voice, she thought ruefully, was thin and strained. He apologised for not meeting them sooner, 'But my doctor doesn't like me exerting myself. I tend to spend a lot of time reading, or resting.'

It didn't sound like a very healthy lifestyle to her, but she nodded politely and moved the conversation on to other things. She chatted about her grandfather, with

Freddie butting in every two minutes with anecdotes which were only just on the right side of *risqué*, and after a while the old man began to look slightly more animated.

'He was a rogue in his youth, that old Jacob,' Sir John said whimsically.

Leigh laughed, throwing her head back, 'He was a rogue in his maturity as well, Sir John, believe me.'

'He drove the women crazy,' Freddie said with a grin.

'He did?'

Leigh nodded. 'There was always some lady or other being invited around for coffee. If he really liked her...'

'He would present her with something he'd made,' Freddie finished. Leigh looked at her brother, and they giggled.

'There was this one lady,' Freddie offered, laughing at the memory until tears came to his eyes, 'Mrs Bolby, a widow.'

'Freddie! Sir John won't want to hear about Mrs Bolby!'

'Pray continue, young man.' He really was looking more animated.

'Mrs Bolby,' Leigh said primly, 'was a very quiet lady...'

'A prude!' Freddie screeched.

'And Grandad saw fit—I don't know what got into him...' She began to giggle uncontrollably.

'To present her with this wooden carving of a bed...' Freddie continued.

'And a lute. He told her they could make sweet music under cover!'

Sir John laughed, wheezing at first, then louder.

Over the exquisite meal of salmon with prawns, Freddie and Leigh regaled him with humorous things their grandfather had done. The old man really seemed to enjoy it, and over coffee he shook his head and murmured how much he envied Jacob's life.

'Having you two must have been a source of delight to him. Of course, I have Nicholas, and I love him dearly, but he's rarely around and, as for me, I don't get out at all,' he confessed. 'Don't see the point. The world's changed around me, and I don't care for what goes on out there at all.'

'It's not all bad, Sir John,' Leigh said gently, placing her hand over his. She was about to tell him all about her beautiful countryside, the free, enticing nature that surrounded her in Yorkshire, when the door opened and she turned around, her eyes fixed on Nicholas, who was dressed formally, in a charcoal-grey suit, his black hair swept back from his face.

Then she saw that there was someone behind him. A woman. She stepped into the sitting-room and Leigh gasped because she was quite simply the most stunning creature she had ever seen.

She was tall and voluptuous, all the curves in exactly the right places, and she clearly was aware of that fact, because her black dress curved lovingly and tightly around her body, plunging at the front to reveal more of her cleavage than Leigh would have thought possible.

She was only wearing one thick gold chain, but even so there was something expensive about her. Nothing you could quite put your finger on, but the overall package was chic beyond belief. The severely cut short black hair, the large dark eyes, the perfectly proportioned face with more than a hint of coldness about it.

Leigh had a sharp, terrible thought: Nicholas obviously doesn't find her cold. And she obviously was very warm indeed around him because when she glanced at him there was something positively simmering about her.

'You're up late, Sir John,' she said, moving gracefully into the room on very, very high heels. She looked straight at Leigh and threw her a smile which somehow succeeded in being disdainful rather than friendly. Her eyes travelled quickly over her, and registered that there was no threat there.

'Leigh and Freddie,' Nicholas introduced, sitting on the sofa and stretching out his long legs in front of him, 'this is Lady Jessica Thompson.' He began tugging at his tie, pulling it down until he was able to undo the top button of his shirt.

'Pleased to meet you,' Leigh said warmly, standing up and stretching out her hand, which Lady Jessica took briefly and then dropped as though finding the exercise thoroughly boring.

Freddie was a little wiser. He said, 'Hi,' from the sidelines, but made no effort to shake Lady Jessica's hand and exited from the party as soon as he possibly could.

Leigh fervently wished that she could do the same, but when she attempted to do so Sir John gestured her back into her seat, and instead eased himself up, rejecting Nicholas's offer of help.

'Oh, do help him up, darling,' Lady Jessica murmured, and was rewarded with something that sounded remarkably like a snort from Sir John. 'You know how frail your poor grandfather is.'

Sir John winked at Leigh slyly and her lips twitched.

'Are you ready for bed, Grandfather?' Nicholas asked, ignoring Lady Jessica's suggestion.

'I am now,' Sir John said.

Nicholas and Sir John both vanished from the room, and Leigh remained perched on the edge of her chair, rooting around in her mind for something to say, although from the look of the other woman there was very little that she was prepared to find interesting in Leigh's conversation.

'Nicholas told me all about you,' Lady Jessica said, crossing her slim legs, and flicking an invisible fleck of dust from her stocking. 'And I must say, you look so much younger than I expected. My dear, how do you do it? You hardly look a day over fourteen.'

It was all Leigh could do to remember that she was a guest in the house and that she should be polite to her host's friends.

She gritted her teeth and smiled politely. 'Really?' she said evenly. 'I'm not sure whether to take that as a compliment, but I will anyway.'

'Oh, my dear, of course it's a compliment!' Lady Jessica exclaimed, in a voice which left Leigh in no doubt whatsoever that it wasn't. 'Though, to be brutally honest, it doesn't really—how shall I phrase this?—fit in here in London. You look, well, a bit too young and innocent. Anyone would think you worked here, for heaven's sake, instead of being a guest in the house!'

Leigh's face was beginning to ache from the effort of smiling politely when she would much rather have thrown her cup of cold coffee into Lady Jessica's carefully made-up face.

'My dear——' Lady Jessica's eyes opened wide when there was no response from Leigh '—I do hope you don't think I'm being rude. I only want to help you while you and your brother are here!'

'We'll manage just fine,' Leigh said tightly.

'Of course you will. Silly little me. I simply wanted to warn you that London isn't anything like your little village. It's full of sharks, and it's always just as well to be prepared.'

'I'll bear that in mind.'

'How long do you plan on staying anyway?' Lady Jessica wasn't looking in her direction, but Leigh knew instinctively that it was a loaded question.

She shrugged and said perversely, 'I don't know.'

'Really?' This time she did look at Leigh and her black eyes were as hard as little chips of stone.

Leigh nodded.

'And what do you intend to do about money?' she asked patronisingly. Surely not live off charity, her voice implied.

'Nicholas has offered me a job with him.'

She could see that this was unwelcome news to Lady Jessica, but the other woman recovered her composure quickly. 'That would be Nicholas, of course. Always doing the right thing. I expect he feels so very sorry for you and your brother.' She smoothed her hands along her legs, and continued, 'He always did have a soft spot for the underdog, believe it or not.' She gave a throaty laugh. 'I suppose it has something to do with his profession.'

Leigh felt the blood rush to her hairline.

'If you'll excuse me,' she muttered, getting to her feet, barely able to control the anger raging inside her, 'I want to say goodnight to Freddie, and I'm still quite tired after the long journey, so if you don't mind...' Leigh couldn't care less whether Lady Jessica minded or not, because she knew that if she stayed there a second more she would explode, and that was the very last thing she wanted to do. That would be to reduce herself to the very show of childish ill temper which the other woman was no doubt hoping for.

Oh, no, she would make a very quiet exit, and then pummel her pillow to death in the privacy of her bedroom.

Underdogs indeed! Was that how Mr High and Mighty Nicholas Reynolds saw them? Had he said so to this awful woman? And what else had he told her? That they were destitute, perhaps?

Lady Jessica uncoiled her elegant body from the sofa and stood up, towering over Leigh in her flat shoes.

'Of course,' she murmured in agreement, 'I suppose this must be quite a late night for you, especially with all the excitement of coming down here.'

Really, Leigh thought, did this silly woman imagine that everyone who lived outside London retired to bed promptly at seven o'clock with their cups of Horlicks?

'Yes,' Leigh said, unable to resist a few parting words of sarcasm, 'I can hardly cope.'

She didn't know why she bothered because Lady Jessica looked at her blankly, then she said in a slow, careful voice, 'I shouldn't be too impressed by everything you see here, my dear. And I particularly shouldn't be too impressed by Nicholas. I know he's an extremely attractive man, but you take it from me that the last thing he wants is to be bothered by some wide-eyed innocent becoming infatuated with him.'

Leigh looked at her, speechless. This was the limit.

'And you can take it from me,' she answered in a cool, cool voice which masked her icy anger, 'that the last person in the world I could ever find interesting would be Nicholas Reynolds. I could no more be infatuated with him than I could be with a toad from the bottom of the garden. But thank you so very much for your advice...' She paused and subjected Lady Jessica to one of her own looks of disdain. 'I'm sure every word of it was uttered with my welfare at heart.'

She turned away and swept out of the room, her head held high, her fists clenched at her sides.

She almost collided with Nicholas, who was coming down the stairs.

'Going to bed?' he asked, staring at her flushed face, but not commenting on it.

'We country people need our rest,' Leigh said, her voice taut. 'We're not used to late nights!'

Then she continued walking quickly up the staircase, not slowing down until she was outside her bedroom door.

She didn't think that she had ever been so enraged or so insulted in her whole life. She could feel the anger thudding inside her, with a life of its own.

She was still fuming by the time she was finally under the covers and the lights were switched off, even though she told herself that she was stupid to let anything Lady Jessica said get to her.

She and Nicholas Reynolds richly deserved each other. Both as hard as nails, and ruthless in their own individual ways.

The whole evening, she thought, which had been so enjoyable with Sir John, had been spoilt by Lady Jessica. And, Leigh thought dimly, by Nicholas, because she might as well bracket them together. They were a couple, and that, Lady Jessica had made patently clear, was how she intended it to stay.

Not that she needed to make a point about it. Leigh could have told her for free that Nicholas Reynolds was not her kind of man. If he got under her skin, it was because he was arrogant and so totally out of her league that it was laughable.

And that, she thought dimly as she drifted off to sleep, was precisely how she meant to keep it.

CHAPTER THREE

SIR JOHN, the following morning, was horrified to learn that Leigh intended starting work as soon as possible. He was sitting in front of a plate of toast and honey at the breakfast table and he turned to face his grandson.

'You never told me that you had offered Leigh a job,' he accused.

'Didn't I?' Nicholas sipped from his cup of black coffee and glanced down at his watch.

He was dressed in a charcoal suit, his dark hair swept back from his face, and as Leigh tucked into her plateful of bacon and eggs she eyed him surreptitiously across the table.

He really was flawlessly handsome. Not in a rugged way, but with a certain cold hardness that was emphasised by the perfect chiselling of his features.

Freddie was busily eating, paying scant attention to the conversation around him, his mind dwelling, Leigh suspected, on far more trivial things.

'No, you didn't,' Sir John said testily. 'When did all this take place?'

'When I went up to Yorkshire,' Nicholas replied smoothly. His eyes skimmed across to Leigh and she hurriedly looked down at her plate of food. 'We both felt that it was a good idea for her to work for me,' he was adding, then he paused for a fraction, as if giving her the opportunity to object, which she didn't. 'I've been looking for a replacement for Karen for a few weeks, and Leigh didn't want to feel as though she was accepting charity. Did you?' The grey eyes fixed on her face.

'Charity?' Sir John spluttered. 'My dear, it's a delight having you here. Nothing charitable about it at all.'

'Oh, I know,' Leigh said awkwardly. 'But Nicholas is right——' in a loose manner of speaking, she added to herself '—I want to go out to work. I resigned from my job at the library, and I need the money to put towards the cottage...' Her voice trailed off.

'But you could have spent a bit more time relaxing. When do you plan on starting?'

Leigh looked questioningly at Nicholas, feeling very much like one of the serving staff whose fate lay in the hands of the master of the house.

'Tomorrow?' he asked.

'That'll be fine.' Do I have a choice? she added silently.

'I'll be in all morning, so I can show you the ropes, and then you can take it from there.'

'Fine.'

'But what about Freddie?' Sir John looked at him fondly. 'Won't you miss not seeing the sights with your sister?'

Freddie grinned. 'Hardly. Besides, I could always go with you.'

'Me?' Sir John looked horrified. 'Doctor's orders, son. I'm afraid the outdoor life is a thing of the past for an old man like me. Well, I think it's downright rude to drag this poor child off to work so soon after she's arrived. We've hardly had any time to renew our friendship. It's rare enough that I find someone who doesn't treat me like a half-wit. As some people tend to do.'

There was a little silence, then Nicholas said in a restrained voice, 'I hope this isn't leading where I think it is, Grandfather.'

'Leading?' Sir John looked innocently at his grandson, whose face was a mixture of frustration and impatience. 'Where on earth could it be leading?'

Nicholas sighed and looked very much as though he would have liked to conclude the conversation but was prevented from doing so out of a sense of respect for his grandfather.

'I'm sure Leigh and Freddie don't want to be bored by all this,' he finally said in a heavy voice.

'By all what?' Freddie asked, helping himself to two more slices of bread.

Sir John leaned conspiratorially towards him. 'Nicholas and I disagree on a certain lady,' he said. 'A certain Lady Jessica who treats me like an outpatient from the local mental institution.'

'Grandfather!' Nicholas warned.

Leigh wanted to laugh out loud. She would never have believed that Nicholas could ever look anything but controlled, but right now he was looking decidedly uncomfortable.

'Well, she does,' Sir John complained. 'She talks as though I'm deaf and senile. One of these days I almost expect her to waltz through the front door with a nurse in tow. Leigh doesn't talk to me as though I'm deaf and senile.' He looked fondly at her. 'I remember you when you were a tiny lass,' he mused, 'running about with your pigtails and not a care in the world.'

'I remember running about and pigtails,' she grinned, 'and it wasn't that long ago.'

Nicholas stood up abruptly. 'Well, I really have no time for these charming reminiscences.'

'Do you remember Leigh, son? You two used to play together sometimes.'

Leigh gave him a saccharine-sweet smile and he frowned heavily at her. Lord, she thought, how nice to see him cornered for once.

He thrust his hands into his pockets and said, 'Vaguely, yes.'

'Old Jacob and I—well, old men dream, don't they?' Sir John continued wistfully, ignoring his grandson's discomfort. 'Anyway...' He shook himself out of his reverie and looked fondly at her. 'If you're planning on starting work tomorrow, and there's no way that I can talk you out of it, at least do me the honour of visiting London on my behalf, and I would be delighted if you would make full use of my Harrods chargecard. I know what you're going to say——' he waved aside her protests '—but it would make an old man happy.'

'I really can't,' Leigh began awkwardly, aware that Nicholas was watching their interchange with sharp interest.

'Please. For me. I know if the positions had been reversed, Jacob would have done the same for my grandson.'

'But they're not, are they?' Nicholas observed smoothly.

'Nicholas,' Sir John said firmly, 'allow an old man his indulgences.'

He looked questioningly at Leigh and she nodded in resignation.

'Leigh, can I see you for a minute before I leave?' Nicholas said acidly.

A warm wave of colour stole over her face. She knew what he wanted, and she was already on the defensive as she followed him into the hall.

He flicked open his briefcase, scanned some papers, then shut it and faced her.

'So,' he bit out, 'would you like to explain what all that was about?'

'All what?' she asked faintly. She could feel that unaccustomed fluttering inside which made her almost want to step backwards—like someone standing too close to a fire.

'What exactly do you take me for? A complete fool?'

'Is it my fault that your grandfather is fond of me?' she asked helplessly. There was no point in pretending that she had no idea what he was talking about. If his tone of voice wasn't explicit enough, she could feel the accusations burning in his cold grey eyes.

'No,' Nicholas agreed coolly, 'it's not your fault that my grandfather is fond of you, but I'm highly dubious of the manner you have of returning that affection.'

'What do you mean?'

'Well, do you normally return affection by accepting someone's chargecard?'

His pale eyes bored into her until she felt dizzy from the effort of trying to think straight.

'Of course not!' she snapped.

'Is that because the opportunity has never arisen?'

'How dare you?'

'Spare me the histrionics, please.'

'Only if you spare me the constant insults!' she retorted, her colour high.

'Oh, do forgive me,' he said with effusive sarcasm, 'how could I even dream of it? I mean, here you are, in the lap of luxury, thanks to my dear grandfather, and now in happy possession of an unlimited bank balance. How unusual that it might have crossed my mind that you may just be taking advantage of his fondness for you.'

'I'm not doing anything of the sort,' Leigh objected. Put like that, though, she could well see his point of view and she blushed guiltily.

'But I see from the expression on your face that you get the general drift of what I'm saying?'

He doesn't miss a thing, does he? she thought angrily. Except in this instance, he was way off target—not that there was much chance of convincing him of that. He had not wanted her around in the first place so why should he suddenly decide now to give her the benefit of the doubt?

'That doesn't mean that you're right,' she muttered, unable to summon up much conviction in her voice.

'I'm merely looking at the facts and drawing logical conclusions from what I see.'

'And you're never wrong?'

She stared at him with antagonism and as he looked back down at her she suddenly felt her pulse begin to race. She edged fractionally away from him, disturbed at her reaction to his nearness. He was treating her with despicable arrogance, she told herself in horror, yet here I am acting as though he's about to kiss me.

'Very rarely,' he said silkily. He leaned against the banister and continued to stare at her.

'Well, what a fortunate person you are to go through life with such certainty that you can't put a foot wrong,' she bit out. 'I pity that poor girlfriend of yours. I can't imagine what she sees in someone as cold and as clinical as you!'

She stopped, aghast at what she had just said.

'Can't you?' he asked softly. He suddenly reached out and stroked the side of her face, an action which assumed the proportion of deep intimacy, and gave a low laugh.

Leigh jerked back, her head spinning at the warmth that had spread through her body at his touch. She knew what he was trying to prove. She might be from the back of beyond, a country girl with no experience in the guiles of high city life, but that didn't mean she was an idiot. Oh, no. That careless gesture was his lazy way of informing her without words that the female sex was more than satisfied with what he could provide.

And she was furious because he had elicited precisely the sort of reaction from her that he had no doubt expected to. She had flinched as though burnt, and she knew that she was breathing quickly, painfully.

His fingers trailed along her collarbone then spiralled down towards the shadowy valley between her breasts, and her breath caught in her throat. Under her blouse, her breasts felt suddenly heavy. She wanted him to go further, she thought with dismay, and she drew back in horror, but his hand had already left her body and was now safely ensconced in the pockets of his trousers.

'I suppose you think that was funny,' she said, trying to control the tremor in her voice. 'Well, you'll have to excuse me if I don't appreciate those sort of urbane city games!'

She folded her arms protectively across her chest, an unconscious gesture which made him raise one eyebrow in amusement.

'What sort of games do you prefer?'

'I prefer honesty between people,' she said in a raised voice. 'And I prefer trust.' She was trembling, and she clenched her fists tightly, determined to draw this conversation away from the personal. Next to his unexpected onslaught of manipulated charm, his arrogance was like a breath of fresh air.

'I'm not taking advantage of Sir John,' she repeated, feeling immediately safer now that the lines of hostility were redrawn between them. 'I have no intention of using his chargecard. I accepted because it was offered in a generous spirit, and to have refused would have been unnecessarily churlish. That doesn't mean that I'm about to go on a wild spending spree!'

'You might as well avail yourself of it,' Nicholas informed her in a vaguely bored tone of voice.

He's said his piece, she thought sourly, he's played his little game, and now he can't wait to get to work. His boredom threshold with me must be remarkably small.

She had a sudden vision of Lady Jessica, with her haughty elegance. She doubted that he tired of her with such speed. They lived in the same world. He could probably spend all the hours God made in her company. Well, she thought, I'm damn well not going to vanish just because he's suddenly decided that he wants to be on his way.

'What do you mean I might as well avail myself of it?' she asked frozenly.

'Well,' he said, scanning her slender frame with embarrassing thoroughness, 'you'll have to invest in some more clothes.'

'What?' She looked at him blankly. What was wrong with her clothes?

'Clothes,' he said, enunciating his words carefully, as though he were speaking to someone hard of hearing. 'You'll have to buy some more.'

Leigh felt a spurt of anger. Not only had he seen fit to blackmail her down here, but he was now dictating to her what she could and could not wear!

'Why?' she asked abruptly. 'What's wrong with my clothes?'

'They're charming,' he drawled, with infuriating calm, 'but they're not nearly businesslike enough for your job in Chambers.'

'You can't tell me what I should wear,' she said mutinously.

'I can and I do.' His voice was low and smooth and faintly dangerous. 'Don't forget, you work for me now.'

'And you're determined to extract every ounce of blood.'

'Can you blame me?'

The grey eyes stared down at her, not releasing her from their hypnotic hold, and it struck her again how easy it was to understand the speed with which he had climbed in his profession. There was something ruthless about him, which could just as quickly give way to that seductive charm which he had exercised on her for his own private amusement. She had not liked it, but, much as she loathed to admit it, he had proved his point admirably.

'Blame you?' she asked innocently. 'How could I even think of doing that when you're never wrong?'

This time there was genuine enjoyment in his eyes when he laughed. It transformed the contours of his face from cold arrogance to warm sensuousness, and Leigh turned away abruptly.

'If I don't see you later,' he informed her, reaching for his briefcase, 'I'll see you in Chambers tomorrow. I have a very early appointment so you'll have to make your own way there.' He gave her brief, clipped instructions of how to get there, and she nodded, frantically hoping that she would remember what he had said, because she knew that he had no intention of repeating himself.

She spent the rest of the day in Knightsbridge trying to put the disturbing image of Nicholas to the back of her mind. It kept popping up, though. In between the clothes rails, in the changing-rooms, at the coffee-bar in the store. Like an unwelcome virus, she thought ill-humouredly.

Still, she managed to get some shopping done. The minimum, because, despite Nicholas's bored permission, she could not bring herself to spend someone else's money liberally. Her pride was too strong for that. So she invested in some items of clothing that could be mixed and matched, and which looked relatively smart.

And if he doesn't think they're suitable, she thought as she nervously dressed for work the following morning, then he could go take a running jump from the nearest very high bridge. The thought brought a smile to her lips which lasted all the way in to work, and only gave way to that sick, nervous feeling in the pit of her stomach when she made it to the office.

Nicholas was nowhere around, and she allowed herself to be taken in hand by one of the clerks, her brain working overtime as she frantically followed everything he told her, only asking questions when absolutely necessary.

'You'll do,' the older man said with a smile, as she returned from the law library in the Chambers with an armful of reference books.

'Will I?' Leigh asked anxiously, and he gave her a reassuring nod.

She expelled a long sigh of grateful relief and grinned. He couldn't begin to know how much his confidence in her abilities meant to her. This was no ordinary job. This was a job in which she would prove her efficiency if it killed her in the process. There was no way that Nicholas was going to have the dubious satisfaction of dismissing her on grounds of incompetence.

By the end of the day, she felt pleasantly tired, but as the rest of her colleagues began heading for the door she shook her head with a laugh.

'You've all got a head start on me,' she pointed out with a smile. 'I need to work some overtime so that I don't slow you all down.'

'Not such a bad idea,' Frank, the old man who had shown her the ropes agreed. 'Nicholas might be all sunshine and light with you out of work, but in here he's a hard taskmaster. He never stops and he never expects anyone to either.'

Leigh grinned feebly at him. Sunshine and light? What a joke. There was more sunshine and light in the Arctic on a cold winter night.

She watched them depart, and then refocused her attention on the workload, only looking up when the outer door opened with a click.

Nicholas was the last person she was expecting. She had seen nothing of him all day, and she had blissfully assumed that he would not be putting in an appearance at all. So her eyes widened in shock as she took in his tall, powerful body framed in the doorway.

'Still here?' he asked, striding into the room, which suddenly seemed to have become alarmingly claustrophobic.

Leigh ventured a light laugh. 'There's a lot to learn,' she said vaguely.

'You should try it from where I'm standing,' he replied grimly, raking his fingers wearily through his hair. 'Come into my office,' he said, walking through and expecting her to follow. She rose quickly and trailed behind him, wishing now that she had left slightly earlier.

The office felt even more claustrophobic than the outside room. He seemed to dwarf it with his presence. She watched as he strolled towards the window and stared absent-mindedly down into the street below.

You look as though you've had one hell of a day, she wanted to say.

'I'm thoroughly enjoying the job so far,' she volunteered, to break the silence, and he turned to face her.

'Something of a change from your job at the library?' he asked.

'Slightly,' Leigh agreed. 'Although I don't seem to have escaped the presence of books.'

'Been running to and from the reference library?'

'Something like that.'

'Sorry I wasn't around today,' he began, perching on his desk, and rubbing his eyes with his fingers. 'In this business, things don't always go according to plan.'

'That's quite all right,' Leigh said hurriedly, 'Frank has been more than helpful.' There was a short silence. 'Perhaps you ought to go home,' Leigh finally suggested. 'You look as though bed's the best place for you at the moment.'

'Depends on who's in it with me,' Nicholas murmured lazily, and she blushed. 'Actually,' he continued in a brisker voice, 'I have to clear a few things up here. How much longer are you going to be? I can give you a lift back.'

'A lift?'

'In the car.'

'Sure,' she said with a sinking feeling, 'a lift back in the car. That sounds great. I'll be another half-hour or so, but don't worry if you want to stay longer. It's no problem. I'm quite capable of making the journey back on the Underground.'

His eyes narrowed on her. 'Anyone would think that you were trying to avoid my company,' he drawled. 'Half an hour will be fine. Now, I have a list of files I need you to dig up for the first thing tomorrow morning.' He pulled out a sheet of paper and handed it to her. 'Do you think you can handle that?'

'I think so,' she responded sweetly. 'I don't suppose I need a degree in nuclear physics to find my way round a filing system.'

Something like amusement flashed across his face, without actually surfacing into a smile.

She stood up, ready to leave before this unexpected truce between them was broken.

'I see you did some shopping,' he commented, stretching back in his chair, his hands clasped behind his head.

Leigh glanced down at her outfit self-consciously. It was a simple straight skirt in a grey-blue colour which she had worn with a man's styled pin-striped shirt. Not the sort of thing that she was accustomed to wearing, but then, as he had more or less pointed out, a library in Yorkshire was hardly the same thing as Chambers in London.

She waited for the inevitable sarcasm, the re-instatement of cold war.

'It's very appropriate,' he murmured, and she eyed him warily. Not quite the insult she was expecting, but then, she had realised, innocuous remarks from him often had a way of turning into biting criticisms. A tactic he no doubt employed in court.

'I thought so,' she ventured evenly.

'Suits you. Makes you look more severe, though. Especially with you hair knotted back like that. There's something desperately tempting about hairstyles like that.'

She watched, frozen to the spot, as he moved swiftly across to her, his hand reaching behind her to release her carefully prepared chignon.

Her heart was beating heavily in her chest, and she had to take deep breaths to control her emotions, which seemed to be running haywire all of a sudden.

'There,' he murmured with satisfaction, 'that looks infinitely better.'

Her hair flowed around her, a mass of tumbling red. Matching my face, she thought. He's doing it again. Playing with me for a spot of amusement. She parted her lips to give him a swift retort when the door behind them opened and Leigh spun around to see Lady Jessica standing there, her eyes taking in everything, from the proximity of their bodies to the hectic colour in her cheeks.

Nicholas didn't look in the slightest bit put out by the appearance of his girlfriend. Nor, Leigh noticed, did he make any effort to move back to the security of his desk. No, it was up to her to put some distance between them, which she did, very hurriedly.

Lady Jessica viewed Leigh with dislike and then spoke, her voice hard and brittle.

'Doing some overtime on your first day here? How industrious.'

Nicholas was once more seated on the edge of the desk, his arms crossed, his face betraying nothing whatsoever.

Leigh smiled weakly and watched as the other woman moved gracefully across the room to Nicholas, and draped her arm around his neck. Staking her claim, Leigh thought drily. Can't she see that she has no need to bother?

'Nick, darling,' Lady Jessica said, resting her chin comfortably on his shoulder, 'you hadn't forgotten that I was going to meet you here, had you?'

'As a matter of fact I had,' he drawled, watching Leigh as he spoke.

'You naughty boy!' She ran her long white fingers through her hair and he abruptly rose to his feet.

'Haven't you got work to be doing?' Lady Jessica directed the question to Leigh. 'Can't you see that we want to be alone together?'

Leigh's face managed a polite smile. 'I'll do that reference work before I leave,' she said, looking at Nicholas and all the time aware of the hostility flowing out of the other woman. He nodded briefly, and she turned on her heels and fled.

You're acting like a fool, she told herself disparagingly, as she rifled through the bookshelves and withdrew the appropriate law books. Anyone would think that I'd been caught at the scene of a crime instead of in the boss's office quite innocently getting some work.

Except, she thought, I didn't feel that innocent, did I?

The question hovered on the edge of her mind, daring her to explore it further, and, hard as she tried to fight it, she found herself reliving those minutes in his office, reliving that sickening sense of attraction she had felt when he had stood inches away from her, his hand in her hair.

She dumped the reference books on her desk and began flicking through the pages, marking the relevant chapters, but her brain was buzzing with unwelcome thoughts.

So, she told herself, she had found him attractive. For just that split second. He was an attractive man. He had that lethal combination of brains and good looks that few women would be able to resist.

And it was late. She had been working hard all day. He had caught her with her defences down. That was it, of course. It had all been a question of the wrong place at the wrong time, and she should be grateful that Lady Jessica had interrupted things when she had, because she had a feeling that that momentary attraction which she had felt for him might have become a little too embarrassingly obvious.

She glanced across to the closed office door and moved tentatively towards it.

Now that Lady Jessica was here, there was no way that she was going to hang around for a lift back, but she refused to be cowed into simply running away without letting him know of her decision.

She hesitatingly approached the door and was about to knock when she heard her name being spoken. She stopped, torn between a desire to leave and an insatiable curiosity to find out what was being said about her.

Lady Jessica's voice was low but piercing, rising and falling.

'I knew it was a mistake taking her on here, Nicholas,' she heard Lady Jessica say with malevolence. 'In fact, it was a huge mistake bringing her down to London in the first place just through some absurd whim of your grandfather's. She doesn't belong here.'

Leigh's body was shaking with anger, but her feet remained glued to the spot.

'She's a cheap gold-digger, we both know that,' Lady Jessica continued in a rush, 'and, worse than that, if you're not careful, she's going to try and get her claws into you.'

There was deep laughter, then Lady Jessica's voice returned with increased anger. 'You might laugh, but . . .' Her voice lowered, and Leigh turned away quickly, feeling sick.

She found her bag and blindly made her way out of the building.

Why, she wondered furiously, was she so disturbed by what she had heard? Didn't she already know what Nicholas thought of her? Hadn't he made that obvious enough? So now she knew that Lady Jessica shared his low opinion. That should hardly surprise her.

Those two, she thought, richly deserved each other. She could well imagine them laughing at her, comparing notes on what little schemes they thought she had in mind for getting her hands on the family fortune.

It's beneath contempt, she thought. But inside her head a little voice was warning her to be careful, because she had a suspicion that Lady Jessica would stop at nothing to protect her investment in Nicholas. And that same little voice was telling her that Lady Jessica could be very dangerous indeed.

CHAPTER FOUR

LEIGH buried herself in her work for the remainder of the week. She also avoided doing any overtime unless she was absolutely certain that Nicholas was not going to be around.

It's not as though I don't trust myself, she thought with uneasy rationalisation, it's simply that certain situations could not arise if the opportunity was not there in the first place.

Nevertheless, by the time Friday evening rolled around she couldn't help feeling relieved that there had been no more uncomfortable confrontations with him. He had been around, but intermittently, and when he had made an appearance she had resolutely averted her eyes from him and concentrated on her work. Like a schoolgirl who busied herself with her books at the back of the class, and hoped that the teacher would forget her presence.

As she strolled down to breakfast on the Saturday morning, she realised with a twinge of guilt that she had been so wrapped up in her own thoughts, and in the job, that she had barely seen anything of Sir John or Freddie.

They were both waiting for her at the breakfast table, and she greeted them with a broad smile, her conscience making her more garrulous than she normally was.

Freddie, she learned, had just landed himself an apprenticeship, and she made the appropriate exclamations of delight.

'No need to go overboard,' he told her, when she had congratulated him for the third time. 'It's just a job. I don't remember you being so enthusiastic when you got that job with Nicholas.'

'Wasn't she?'

Leigh raised her eyes to see Nicholas approaching them through the kitchen door. Did he have to move so stealthily? she wondered with irritation.

There was a short silence while all eyes turned to her, and she smiled sweetly.

'I was thrilled,' she said, saving a particularly sickly smile for Nicholas, who had sat down opposite her and was pouring himself a cup of coffee. 'If I recall,' she continued, 'it was an offer I couldn't refuse.'

Sir John was watching them closely, then he dropped his eyes and said in a casual voice, 'Freddie and I have already had our little celebration at his job. And I thought that tonight the three of us could go to the theatre to celebrate in a more adult fashion.'

Leigh looked at him in amazement.

'You're going to leave the house?' she asked. 'But I thought...'

'Can't stay cooped up in here for the rest of my life,' Sir John informed her. He glanced across at Nicholas, challenging him to say something, but there was silence.

'Anyway, I'm beginning to go a peculiar shade of grey from being indoors too much,' Sir John carried on. 'The doctor never warned me about that side-effect.'

'Since when have you given a damn what shade of colour you were?' Nicholas asked drily. 'Don't tell me that you've decided to become vain in your ripe old age.'

'That's a very unpleasant thing to say,' Sir John replied testily. 'It's never too late to start caring about one's appearance.'

'I see,' Nicholas said thoughtfully. 'Well, Grandfather, I'm afraid the two of you will have to go on your own. I've made other arrangements for this evening, and——'

'With that awful woman, I suppose?' Sir John interjected disapprovingly.

'Not this again.' There was an edge of impatience to his voice which Sir John ignored.

'I'm an old man...'

'So you keep reminding us...'

'With few pleasures left in life...'

'I don't know. You seem to have rediscovered the value of mirrors...'

Leigh stifled her amusement and bit into her piece of toast and marmalade.

'I never thought I'd see the day that my own grandchild would poke fun at my expense.' Sir John shook his head sorrowfully and darted a sidelong glance at Leigh from under his bushy brows. 'I would have thought that you of all people, Nicholas, would have been delighted...'

'Believe me, I am, Grandfather...' He was beginning to get that cornered look which Leigh had come to recognise in his dealings with his grandfather.

'...at my decision to leave the house,' Sir John went on. 'Of course, I can see now that you're all too happy to have me remain here, trapped between these walls, never breathing the fresh air——'

'The air in London is hardly fresh,' Nicholas interrupted, adopting another tactic.

'Why else——' Sir John turned to face Leigh '—would he cast aside my pathetic decision to go out to the theatre tonight in favour of some jaunt with that awful woman?'

Leigh cleared her throat and smiled weakly. She didn't want to be part of this interchange, but Sir John was looking at her, expecting some kind of response.

She shrugged and glanced across to Nicholas. 'Perhaps he'd rather spend the time with Lady Jessica,' she said placatingly. Wrong words. Nicholas frowned heavily at her.

'I really don't think you're qualified to make sweeping assumptions on my motives for doing anything,' he retorted coldly.

Why not? she was tempted to ask. You do about mine. She stared blankly at him until he clicked his tongue impatiently.

'Well, maybe she's right, Nicholas,' Sir John murmured with a sigh. 'Maybe you would rather spend time with that awful woman than with your frail old grandfather...'

'Oh, all right!' Nicholas snapped, and was rewarded with a beaming smile from Sir John. 'Where are we going?'

Sir John named a popular romantic musical playing in Shaftesbury Avenue. 'I've already bought the tickets,' he informed them. 'Starts at seven. I thought we could go and then perhaps have a bite to eat afterwards.'

That settled, he returned to his breakfast with gusto, only briefly glancing at Nicholas as the latter excused himself a few minutes later. They heard the front door slam in the distance and Sir John wiped his mouth delicately with his napkin.

'You'll have to excuse me too, my dear,' he said to Leigh, who was amused to see Freddie spring to his feet as well, his arm fondly around Sir John's shoulders. 'But about tonight. Do go and buy something charming. It's a rather dressy occasion, and I have a delightful necklace I'd like you to have. Belonged to my late wife. Been sitting up there in her jewellery box ever since she departed this vale of tears, and I can't think of anyone I'd rather have it than you, my dear.'

Leigh opened her mouth to protest, and he stopped her before she could utter a syllable.

'Humour me,' he said with a kindly expression, and she understood how Nicholas must feel when faced with his grandfather's opposition.

Seventy-nine years old, she thought wryly, as they left the breakfast-room, and still more than capable of running rings around us all. Still, a trip to the theatre would be fun. Even if Nicholas was going to be there as well. At least she wouldn't have to make conversation with him during the musical, and afterwards, well, Sir John would dilute the intensity of his presence.

She threw herself into buying something wickedly appropriate, finally finding the perfect little black dress at one of the larger department stores in Knightsbridge. The sort of dress which she would never in a million years have bought in Yorkshire, because the opportunity to wear it would have been precisely nil.

Later that evening, as she dressed for the theatre, she looked at her reflection in the mirror with satisfaction.

The dress was long-sleeved and not particularly short, but it clung to her figure lovingly. She slipped on the diamond necklace which Sir John had given her earlier on, despite her further attempts to refuse it, and stood back to survey herself.

She felt like Cinderella about to go to the ball. No prince, of course, and in the morning she would be back to her normal self, but just now it was a wonderful feeling.

She ran lightly down to the sitting-room and pushed open the door, her eyes immediately drawn to Nicholas.

He was standing by the open marble fireplace, a drink in his hand. Something about him, his dark, compelling good looks, made her breath catch in her throat. Then she turned away quickly, hiding her reaction with a polite smile.

'Ready?' she asked brightly.

'My dear,' Sir John murmured, 'you look radiant. Wonderful. Doesn't she, Nicholas?'

'You're not dressed!' Leigh exclaimed in dismay.

'Sadly, I won't be coming with you two,' Sir John informed her, and out of the corner of her eye she saw Nicholas's scowl blacken.

'Why not?' she asked desperately. I can't face an evening on my own with your grandson, she wanted to scream.

'I don't feel very well, I'm afraid.'

'You'll feel better once you're outside,' Leigh pleaded, realising that her objections were pointless. He shook his head.

'Another time. Now, you two go and enjoy yourselves.'

'But...'

Nicholas dumped his glass on the coffee-table and walked across to her. 'Come on,' he said with a grim expression, 'there's no point trying to persuade Grandfather to come. I've spent the past half-hour doing just that and it's got me precisely nowhere.'

Sir John waved cheerily at him, unperturbed by Nicholas's ill humour.

'I won't wait up,' he said lightly. 'Take your time. I've booked your table at the restaurant. Nicholas knows it. See you later.'

Leigh found herself being hustled out of the front door, and as her brain began to get back into gear she stopped in her tracks and turned to Nicholas, her hands on her hips.

'Will you stop acting as though I'm to blame for your grandfather's illness?' she snapped.

Nicholas turned to face her, his face taut.

'Illness? Don't be such a damned fool! He never had any intention of going to the theatre with us.'

'Well, you can't blame me for that!' Leigh stared at him angrily.

'Can't I?' he grated. 'You haven't exactly discouraged him, have you?' He glanced down at her necklace and frowned. 'And where the hell did you get this?'

Leigh stared at him without speaking.

'I see,' he muttered grimly. 'More little presents.'

He turned away and began striding towards the taxi which had been ordered for them, holding the door open for her, then slamming it shut after he had eased himself inside.

Leigh stared at his averted profile with a mixture of anger and defiance. What was the point in trying to protest her innocence? Whatever she said he would twist to suit his own arguments, anyway.

They drove in silence. The taxi deposited them directly outside the theatre, and she followed as he took charge of the tickets, which were for prime seats.

The place was buzzing with people. She stared around her, impressed. A far cry from a barn dance at the village hall, she thought drily. These people were having a night out on the town, and they had dressed for the occasion. The women were chic and impeccably groomed, their eyes skimming over the crowds, covertly eyeing what their rivals were wearing. She noticed that quite a few of those covert glances stopped in their tracks when they saw Nicholas before resuming their restless appraisal of the crowd.

She hurried behind him as he cut through the masses of people milling around, and wondered whether he was as aware of the effect he had on the opposite sex as she was. If he was, he was doing a good job of concealing it. But chances were that he wasn't, she thought. When you were surrounded by that sort of thing all the time, you grew immune to it. The novelty wore off.

They reached their seats and Leigh sat down, peering delightedly around her.

'This is wonderful,' she breathed, turning to face him.

There was a glint of amusement in his eyes as he looked at her. What a rustic he must think I am, it flashed through her head. Shame I didn't wear a little flowered smock, a straw hat, and a twig in my mouth.

'I take it you haven't been to the theatre before?' he asked lazily.

'My little village isn't exactly overflowing with them,' she agreed wryly. 'Good pubs, yes, and wonderful scenery, but nothing like this. I know you're probably wishing that you weren't here, but I'm glad I came.' She could hear the note of defensiveness in her voice, and wondered whether he could as well.

'I'd rather not have been blackmailed by a wily old man into being here,' he murmured, 'but, now that I am here, I suppose I might as well sit back and enjoy it.'

'How good of you,' Leigh said sarcastically. 'Please don't feel obliged to stay here on my account. I'm perfectly capable of looking after myself if you want to leave.'

'Are you?' His eyes roamed over her body. 'Dressed like that? The men in Yorkshire may be immune to that sexy dress you're wearing, but you might find the going a little bit heavier here in London.'

Leigh went bright red. He had not commented on her choice of clothes, and now she wished that he hadn't, because his words threw her into a state of addled confusion.

She searched in her head for something to say that would rescue her from her discomfort and muttered coldly, 'Not everyone has sex on the brain.'

'And you think I do, do you?'

Oh, lord, Leigh thought desperately. Despite what he might think of her as a cold-blooded gold-digger, who was deliberately taking advantage of her situation, nothing had ever prepared her for a conversation along these lines. She simply didn't know how to handle it. She didn't know how to handle *him*.

And, of course, the damned musical was inconsiderately showing no signs of getting into action.

'Don't you?' she asked stiffly, pleased that her voice did not betray her.

He shrugged. 'We act according to our situation, don't we?' he said softly. 'Commitment isn't on my list of priorities, so I don't indulge in it.'

'How controlled.'

His face hardened imperceptibly. 'I don't think I care for the judgemental tone of voice,' he grated. 'As I said, we act according to our situation.' He reached out, and his fingers lingered on the diamond necklace around her neck. Where he touched her, her skin burnt. 'Look at you,' he said coolly. 'Plucked from your good pubs and wonderful scenery, and introduced to all this. Don't tell me you haven't reacted accordingly. This diamond necklace tells its own story.'

She pulled away from him, angry. 'Whatever story it's telling you, it's the wrong one,' she snapped, her eyes cold.

There was a burst of music, as the orchestra finally swung into action, and she turned away in relief.

This, she thought, was going to be heavy weather. She couldn't cope with Nicholas's faces. One minute ruthlessly critical, then charming almost without trying. Until, that was, he remembered his mistrust of her, then that cold mask would snap into place, leaving her bewildered and confused.

The thoughts raged through her head, until they were driven back by the players on the stage, acting out their absorbing tale of thwarted love. By the time the curtain fell for the intermission, she found that she had been enjoying herself.

'Drink?' Nicholas asked, rising to his feet.

She nodded, her eyes still bright from the pleasure aroused by the play. He guided her to the bar, which seemed much too small for the throng of people occupying it and which was humming with the sound of raised voices. She stood in one corner while he went to fetch their drinks, looking around her in fascination.

He returned and handed her her glass of orange juice, which she gulped thirstily.

'Are you enjoying the play?' she ventured conversationally, and he shrugged.

'Romantic musicals aren't exactly my cup of tea, but yes, it's well done.'

'And what exactly are your cup of tea? Don't tell me, hard-hitting court-room dramas.'

His face softened into an expression of amusement. 'That would be akin to a busman's holiday, wouldn't it? No, I prefer to leave the court-room drama for the court.'

He swallowed a mouthful of whisky, and was about to continue when a tall blond man tapped him on the shoulder, his blue eyes fixed on Leigh.

'Nicholas,' the man said, still staring at Leigh until she averted her eyes. 'Where's Jessica?'

Nicholas didn't miss a thing. He glanced across to Leigh and frowned. 'Not here,' he said succinctly, in a voice which would deter all but the thickest skinned.

'And who might this delightful creature be?' the man asked, undeterred, grinning at Leigh infectiously. 'I, by the way, am Gerry. A friend of a friend of Nicholas.'

Nicholas introduced them shortly, and immediately Gerry insinuated himself next to her.

'An awful place to meet,' he murmured, gesturing to the crowds, and she nodded in agreement.

'Crowded, isn't it?' she said, liking him instantly.

Next to her, she could feel Nicholas's reproving silence.

'We'll have to do something about that,' Gerry said, flirting outrageously.

'Will we?'

'Sure. This is no place to get to know someone.' A wicked smile lit up his face.

She had no difficulty in picking up the signals which he was sending her. Gerry was a playboy through and through. It showed in his flamboyant clothing, pale trousers with an off-white silk shirt and a deep burgundy bow-tie, and in the bantering tone of his voice.

Leigh smiled back at him and could almost feel Nicholas tense next to her.

'Perhaps we could remedy that...' There was the merest hint of a question in his voice.

'Perhaps not,' Nicholas said smoothly. He polished off the remainder of his drink and grasped her elbow.

'I'd love to,' Leigh said, ignoring him. Why should he tell her what she could and could not do? He wasn't her guardian, for heaven's sake.

Gerry looked delighted. 'Can I call you?' he asked, and she nodded.

'Sure,' she agreed as the bells went and she found herself being dragged back to her seat by Nicholas.

The minute the play resumed, she instantly forgot about Gerry. From her brief meeting with him, she had liked him well enough, but he had not made sufficient impact on her to occupy her thoughts. Very few people possessed that immediate force of impact which ensured their place in your consciousness after a first meeting. Most were easily forgotten and it was only through repeatedly seeing them that you built up a steady awareness of them.

By the time they made it out of the theatre, she had all but forgotten Gerry's existence, and Nicholas made no mention of him as they drove towards the restaurant which had been booked by Sir John.

It was a cosy Italian place where the waiters were attentive without being obsequious, the décor tasteful and elegant, and the prices horrifyingly astronomical.

No doubt adhering to his decision that he might as well enjoy himself, now that he was stuck with her, Nicholas chatted to her about the play, his manner easy and relaxed. Although, she noticed, there was always something vaguely watchful about him when he was with her.

Leigh refused to let that deflate her. She sipped her wine, allowed it to go to her head, and heard herself chatting back to him without her normal defences inhibiting her.

There was something strangely unreal about being here, dining on fine food, and drinking superb wine. Like some sort of dream.

She smiled at him and he met her eyes.

'A private joke?'

'No joke,' Leigh said seriously, 'I was just thinking how much I enjoyed the musical. It was terribly romantic, wasn't it?'

'Unrealistic, I would have said,' Nicholas remarked drily.

'That's a very pragmatic reaction.' She nibbled on her starter of smoked salmon and looked at him. The two glasses of wine were beginning to go to her head, knocking down her usual guarded reaction to him, and she thought with alarming clarity that he really was devastatingly sexy.

'It's the best way to be,' he drawled, staring back at her until she lowered her eyes.

'Is it?'

'Of course. Only a fool allows himself to be swept off his feet by something as unreliable as love. If such a thing exists. Frankly I have my doubts. From what I've seen, people's motivations are usually far more materialistic.'

Leigh swallowed another tiny mouthful of wine and felt a rush of heady excitement.

'That's rather hard.'

'But true. Most people are out for what they can get, even if that something is just the desire to persuade themselves that happiness and security are attainable.'

'And they're not?'

'Look at the divorce rate.'

She looked at him furtively and found his eyes on her. My God, she thought, you're too attractive for your own good. Stop staring at him, she told herself sternly, try to remember that you are his adversary. And she did try. Very hard. But the wine had made her thoughts fuzzy.

'That doesn't mean that people don't hope that things will work out for them,' she heard herself saying. 'If everyone thought like you, there would be no such thing as marriage.'

Nicholas's mouth twisted cynically. 'And would that be such a bad thing?'

There was a bitter tone to his voice, and she thought suddenly, He's not speculating at all. He's speaking from experience. Something has tarnished his faith in human nature, and despite what he says it has nothing to do with what he sees every day in court, though that doubtless didn't help.

She found herself burning with curiosity, wanting to know what had shaped his views on life.

It was easy to overlook all the intricate web of events which lay behind the simplest of people's actions, but no one went through life unaffected by interaction. The depth of her desire to know more about Nicholas frightened her in its intensity, and served to snap her out of her mellow mood of relaxation.

To be defensive with him was one thing. Even to find him objectively attractive. But to be genuinely interested in him and in what made him tick was a dangerous luxury and one which she knew instinctively she should avoid.

She sought in her mind for something totally innocuous to say and was saved the effort by the sudden appearance of Gerry at their table. She was so taken aback that she stared at him openly, and he grinned back, obviously misreading her reaction.

'We meet again,' he said, ignoring Nicholas's presence.

'What are you doing here?' Nicholas demanded, and Gerry said good-humouredly,

'Just passing through, would you believe it? No, seriously, I kind of followed you here.' He gazed at Leigh and Nicholas's eyes narrowed on them. 'A difficult exercise in London, but I managed it. Just. Actually, I've been sitting over there——' he pointed to a table in the darkest corner of the room '—working myself up to coming over here. I hope I don't seem forward?' He addressed the question to Leigh, his blue eyes reminding her of a lost little puppy. Freddie sometimes looked that way when he was trying to wheedle his way around her for one reason or another.

'Very,' Leigh said, unable to resist a laugh, and Gerry adopted an expression of horror.

'Does this mean that I won't be able to take you to——' and he named a well-known London nightclub '—tomorrow night?'

'Yes, what does it mean?' Nicholas asked silkily, sitting back in the chair and folding his arms across his chest. 'We're both on the edge of our seats.'

Back to a state of war, Leigh thought, shooting him an angry glance. How could someone change so quickly?

She raised her eyes to Gerry, who was anxiously awaiting her reply. 'I'd love to accompany you tomorrow,' she said evenly, 'just so long,' she warned, 'as you bear in mind I'm a new hand at this.'

Nicholas muttered something under his breath and Leigh ignored him. Why should she let him crawl under her skin and dictate her responses to other people?

Gerry's face had broken into a pleased grin. 'Shall I pick you up around eight?' he asked, and she nodded in agreement, watching in amusement as he jauntily left the restaurant a few minutes later.

Nicholas's face, when she turned to face him, was icy with hostility.

'Are you quite ready to leave?' he asked, watching her as she drained the rest of her coffee.

They left the restaurant in silence, but she might have guessed that it was too good to last. The minute they were in the street, he rounded on her, his face darkly cynical.

'I must say, for someone who professes to be unused to the fast life, you certainly adapt with surprising ease.'

Leigh refrained from commenting. She had a sneaking suspicion that any contribution from her would only serve to fan the fire and, besides, she didn't feel that she owed him any explanation for her actions.

'Well?' he demanded, grasping her by the arm and half dragging her along. She hurried to keep pace with him, her high heels clacking against the pavement.

'Where are you taking me?'

'To get a taxi,' he grated, 'where else? And it's just as well that I'm taking you; God knows who else might take your fancy between here and the house.'

'That's a nasty thing to say,' Leigh said, breathless with rage.

'Well, you certainly weren't backward in giving Gerry the come-on,' Nicholas said coldly.

'I didn't realise that that was what I was doing.'

'Really, lady, who are you trying to kid? In case you don't know, Gerry isn't exactly Mr Stable. He has a new woman every week.'

'Are you trying to warn me off him?' Her breath was coming in little bursts from the exertion of keeping up with his strides.

'Merely informing you of a few facts. Gerry's a playboy. A pretty face with far too much money for his own good. He's an only child, and his parents have always lavished him with whatever he wanted. He's never done a day's work in his life...'

'Thanks for the warning,' she snapped, as they approached a taxi, and he yanked open the door for her. 'You sound like an irate father lecturing to his daughter on the birds and the bees.' She climbed into the cab and felt the seat depress under his weight as he sat alongside her.

He leaned forward to tell the taxi driver where they wanted to go and then sank back, his face hard.

'Do I really?' he said, turning to face her. It was shadowy inside the taxi, and it was difficult for her to make out the expression on his face. All she could see was the glint of his eyes in the darkness.

'You don't own me,' she said quietly. 'You may have got me down here, but that's no reason for you to believe that you can run my life.'

'Oh, I'm not trying to run your life.' His mouth was derisive as he stared across the shadows at her. 'Perhaps I'm worried about Gerry. Has that occurred to you? After all, he's very wealthy.'

His words hung in the air, tempting her to strike back.

'I see. And a good catch is just waiting for a good fisherman. Or should I say fisherwoman? Is that it?' Her voice had risen imperceptibly.

'Would you like my answer to that?'

No, Leigh thought, I would not like your answer, but she had a feeling that she would get one anyway, and it would be one that she would not find particularly palatable. He was going to be way off target, and she would be impatient to argue with him but she would be forced to listen to what he had to say.

His fingers found the curve of her chin and he twisted her to face him, to meet the dark glitter in his eyes.

'You plead innocence, protest prettily that you're as free from guile as the driven snow. But you spend money on my grandfather's chargecard, and wear the expensive trinkets that he lavishes on you. You look around you and that angelic expression of yours, that butter-wouldn't-melt look in your eyes, but you don't exactly dress like an innocent, do you?' His hand found the curve of her breast, and her body froze as she felt him begin to caress the full swell. She wanted desperately to pull away, but a deep inertia had settled over her.

He continued to massage her breast with his hand, rolling his thumb over her nipple which hardened to his touch underneath the stretchy black material.

'No,' he went on, 'you certainly don't dress the part,' but his voice was slightly unsteady now. He undid the tiny buttons and slipped his hand underneath the dress, and she half closed her eyes, horrified at what was taking place between them, but unable to rouse her body to resistance.

She wasn't wearing a bra and his hand found her naked flesh, settling over the ripe warmth of her breast.

'And you certainly don't act the innocent,' he muttered, and Leigh pulled back, disgusted and shocked at how far she had allowed him to go. She must be insane!

'How dare you?' Her voice sounded strangled, even to her own ears.

'Is that what you plan to do to Gerry?' he asked with biting contempt. 'Bat your eyelashes, smile guilelessly, but dress to provoke and act accordingly?'

A white-hot rage flooded her and she raised her hand, only aware of what she was doing when she made contact with his face, and the ringing slap reverberated in the car.

In the rear-view mirror, she saw the taxi driver glance into the back seat and then just as hurriedly glance away. This, she knew he was thinking, was none of his business.

'Don't ever do that again,' he said through gritted teeth.

'And don't you dare ever insult me again!' To think that only a short while before she had actually found herself liking this man, wanting to know more about him. Well, she had learnt this much—she would be a fool to let any momentary lapse get in the way of common sense. 'I'm not asking you to like me, I'm not even asking you to believe me, I'm merely asking you to extend the same politeness towards me as you would to anyone else.'

'Except you're not anyone else, are you?' he snarled. 'You're little Leigh Taylor, and that child who could run rings around my grandfather has grown into a woman who still can. And you're very much mistaken if I'll let you run rings around anyone else.'

'You can't stop me from seeing Gerry,' she whispered defiantly. 'Why won't you believe me when I tell you that I'm not after anyone's money?'

'Why should I? You're a woman, aren't you? It's in your nature to be opportunistic, but don't think that you can pull the wool over my eyes, because you can't.'

CHAPTER FIVE

LEIGH awoke the following morning with a headache and that peculiar lethargy that came when you hadn't slept properly. She half opened her eyes, and then remembered everything that had happened the night before.

Even in the privacy of her bedroom, her face burned with embarrassment and dismay.

How could she? She slipped out of the bed and ran a shower, standing under it and closing her eyes as the fine needles of water washed over her. In her head, her thoughts flitted around, a kaleidoscope of graphic images which refused to be shoved into the background.

She remembered Nicholas's accusations, the contempt in his eyes. But most of all she remembered her response to him when he had touched her, the way her nerves had flared into wild arousal. She had never felt that way with anyone before, and it had terrified her. It terrified her now, just thinking about it.

It was as though she had spent her lifetime in a state of slumber, waiting for the right key to unlock that uncontrollable yearning which she had felt with him.

She groaned and stepped out of the shower, towelling her hair vigorously. It would have been so convenient to be able to blame the whole shameful episode on drink, but she was honest enough to realise that drink had played no part in her craving for him. He had touched her with the lazy mastery of someone well skilled in the art of making love, and she had reacted with a hunger she had never experienced before.

In a way, she thought, it was just as well that he had only been toying with her to prove a point, because, however much that humiliated her, it would have been far worse if they had taken the lovemaking that step further.

She dressed slowly, avoiding looking in the mirror because she didn't want to see what might be staring back at her.

She told herself that her attraction to him was a mistake, but an excusable one. After all, she was totally inexperienced. Her encounters with men had been gauche and superficial. A movie, a kiss, some awkward fumbling, but she had always held back from anything else.

So of course, she reasoned, she would respond to the experience that Nicholas had brought to his lovemaking. She might dislike him, but for a brief while sheer physical attraction had made her forget that.

So what was the problem? she asked herself, much calmer now that she had worked things out in her head. She risked a glance in the mirror and composed her features into a suitably acceptable mask of control.

Face it, she informed the reflection staring back at her, you don't like Nicholas Reynolds. You don't want to like him. He's rude, insulting, and arrogant. Oh, he can turn on the charm when it suits him to prove a point, he can flash one of those smiles that makes his face look quite different, but underneath it all he's ruthless and dangerous and from a world in which you have no part.

Still, her nerves felt very jumpy as she went downstairs. She didn't much care if she bumped into him or not, but she would rather not.

She released a guilty sigh of relief the minute she realised that he was nowhere around.

Sir John was in the kitchen, juggling with the newspaper while trying to eat at the same time. He looked up as she walked in, and smiled.

'Feeling better?' Leigh asked critically, and he nodded, ignoring the dry barb in her voice.

'Much. Must have been an overnight thing. One of these twenty-four-hour bugs.'

'Must have been,' she agreed, sitting down opposite him and helping herself to a cup of coffee.

He abandoned his fight with the newspaper and rested his elbows on the table, staring at her coyly.

'And how did your evening go?' he asked casually, looking away and buttering a piece of toast.

'The play was terrific. Lovely music, nice storyline, and the atmosphere in the theatre was wonderful. There's nothing at all like that where I come from, as you must know. Plays, in my part of the world, are things strictly reserved for children at the end of term.'

He didn't look impressed with her reply and she wanted to grin.

'So you had a good time,' he insisted, after a while, and she nodded obligingly, noticing that he seemed slightly more pleased with that.

'You're looking really well this morning,' she continued. It would be just as well to change the subject now, before it started getting too uncomfortable. She knew Sir John well enough to realise that he didn't beat about the bush when it came to asking direct questions, and direct questions about Nicholas were the last things she wanted to face. 'That twenty-four-hour bug, so called,' she couldn't resist adding, 'seems to have had quite a reviving effect.'

He flashed her a sheepish look. 'Must be the yellow waistcoat,' he murmured agreeably.

'It's very becoming.' In fact, he looked in peak condition, a thousand times better than he had when they had first arrived. Freddie, she knew, had a lot do with that. Having grown up with only their grandfather as a figure of authority, he had found no difficulty in transferring some of that enthusiastic affection to Sir John.

'It's very yellow. But thank you for the thought, my dear. It's a long time since an old man received compliments of any kind.'

'Surely not!'

'Well, the odious Lady Jessica character hardly has anything pleasant to say, and she's the only female I tend to see these days. Maybe I should get a companion in? A female companion? Eh?'

'Maybe you should,' Leigh agreed thoughtfully. 'Someone long and leggy and bursting with compliments.'

Sir John chuckled. 'Not my type, my dear. And just as well. Don't think I could sit through my grandson's sermons on women being after my bank balance.'

There was a pause and she averted her eyes.

'Have I missed something here?' he asked curiously.

'Missed?'

'I may be an old man, but I'm not a blind old man. You looked decidedly uncomfortable just then.'

Wouldn't it be nice to confide in someone? She fiddled with the coffee-cup, twirling it idly in her fingers, watching the patterns formed by the moving brown liquid.

'It's that damned grandson of mine, isn't it?' Sir John pressed.

Leigh shrugged. 'I think,' she said with a mixture of reluctance and resignation, 'that I fall into the category of one of those women after a healthy bank balance. That's what your grandson thinks anyway.'

'He doesn't! Well, I'll soon set him straight on that score.'

Leigh looked at the determined glint in his eyes with alarm.

'Please don't,' she said hurriedly. She could think of only a few things that could be worse than to be accused of being opportunistic, and Sir John setting Nicholas straight was definitely one of them. Besides, she was more than capable of championing her own causes. She had never backed down from a fight, and she wasn't about to start now.

'Pay no attention to what he says, lass,' Sir John said kindly. 'He can be a bit sensitive on some things. Do you remember him at all as a boy?'

Leigh looked up, startled. 'I guess so,' she said slowly, 'sort of. I was very young at the time.'

'Well, I'll let you into a little secret.' He paused. 'You may remember that Nicholas's parents were hardly ever around. My son had business abroad and they spent most of the year travelling.'

She nodded. In fact, she couldn't remember his parents at all, which spoke volumes about the amount of time they spent in Yorkshire.

'Nicholas doesn't know that I'm aware of this episode at all. But one year, they had returned from one of their trips. I can't recall where they had been. Africa?' He frowned. 'Somewhere quite exotic. Anyway, they returned to find that Nicholas had become great playmates with a young girl called Clarissa and her brother.'

Clarissa. Oh, yes, Leigh remembered her well enough. She had been extremely pretty, with flaxen blonde hair which she had envied with childish desperation. Her own red mane had seemed the ultimate in hideousness by comparison.

She grinned inwardly. Clarissa had grown into an overweight young woman. She had married young and now had three children, and her blondeness was now strictly out of a bottle.

'Well,' Sir John was saying, 'they were alarmed. Gave him a pretty rough time about it. He could only have been about twelve or thirteen at the time, at a vulnerable age. They thought that he was too good for the both of them, you see. Wrong side of the tracks and all that. Nicholas stubbornly continued playing with them, but their words had hit home. Adults don't realise what damage they can do to their children, do they?'

'No, they don't,' she agreed. Children picked things up very quickly and stray remarks or criticisms could be committed to memory with an intensity that could last a lifetime. She could still remember with acute vividness the feeling of being ostracised because she and Freddie had no parents.

'Then we all moved down here. He started dating a young girl when he was about sixteen, and they left him in no doubt whatsoever that they disapproved of the relationship. They should have just left it, of course. It would have fizzled out. As it was, they harped and criticised and the whole thing went on for far longer than it should have.' He shook his head at the memory. 'I think it was all a gesture of defiance from Nicholas. Teenagers don't like being preached at by their parents, and he was more strong-willed than most. But criticism over a period of time is like a destructive, steady drip. And the straw that finally broke the camel's back was when he went to university. He met a young woman. Attractive girl, but quite brash. He became madly infatuated with her.'

'Madly infatuated?' That didn't sound like the controlled, cynical man Leigh knew at all. 'What happened?' She hated herself for her voyeuristic curiosity, but she was intrigued.

'Threw him over for someone else. Someone older and very rich. That crystallised his view of women, and since then, well...' He sighed. 'Protects himself, you see. Natural human reaction. And Nicholas can be dauntingly single-minded. Anyway,' he said in a brighter voice, 'I hope I didn't bore you too much with my ramblings?'

'Not in the least,' Leigh assured him as they left the kitchen.

'So——' he threw her a sideways look '—just ignore anything he says on that score. Get to know him. To know is to understand, and to understand is...'

'Yes, well.' She fidgeted uncomfortably. 'I really must be going. I've got some letters...' She smiled weakly.

'Of course, my dear.' He smiled at her indulgently. 'Still, it's nice that you're working with him. Give you an opportunity to see another side of him.'

She threw him another weak smile. Nice? Nice was for normal people. Nice was for little old ladies who baked apple pies. Nice was not for Nicholas Reynolds. And working with him wasn't nice at all. In fact, a tank full of killer sharks was nice in comparison.

Later, back in her own room, she digested what he had told her. Of course, it went some way to explaining his behaviour, but it didn't excuse it. Nothing could excuse the hostility she saw in his eyes.

Luckily she didn't have to face him for the rest of the day, because she knew that she would still feel that tension rip through her the way it did every time he was around, even after what Sir John had told her. He was out, and she had a fair idea where. With Lady Jessica. She, at least, posed no threat to him. He could see her with a clear conscience, knowing that she wasn't out for his money.

She dressed for her date with Gerry, already regretting her impulsive agreement to see him. Lord knew what she had been trying to prove, but as eight o'clock rolled round she found herself wishing that she had not rushed into something she didn't want.

As it turned out, the evening was a success. The nightclub was crowded and throbbing with music. There was an awful lot of dancing and his attentiveness was flattering.

It made a change from Nicholas, whose aggression seemed to throw her into a permanent state of confusion.

She could relax with Gerry without feeling as though too many demands were being made on her. He loved to talk, and she was quite happy to listen. He told her about his family, their house in the country, his broken relationships, and she didn't feel as though there were depths to him which she would have a struggle trying to plumb.

By the time they finally made it back to the house she was pleasantly tired. He kissed her and she returned his kiss lightly, feeling nothing of that gut-wrenching excitement which she had experienced with Nicholas.

In fact, she was slightly surprised to find that over the next week she saw rather more of Gerry than she had expected.

He took her to his favourite restaurants and he didn't pressurise her into a physical relationship which she knew with increasingly certainty that she didn't want. She enjoyed his company and that was as far as she was prepared to take it.

And it helped that she was in a good frame of mind. Nicholas was not around either at work or at home. She worked hard during the day and relaxed in the evenings, relieved that she didn't have to face him.

This, she thought, as she began clearing her desk in preparation for going home, was much more like how she was normally: calm, controlled, in charge of her life.

She had become so accustomed to not seeing Nicholas that when she heard the outer door click open she didn't even look around. She was working late and there was no one else in the office, but she merely assumed that it was the cleaner.

'Still here?'

The deep voice made her jump and the stack of papers which she had been holding crashed to the floor. She looked around to see Nicholas standing in the doorway, his eyebrows arched.

'I wasn't expecting you,' she replied, angry with herself for her body which suddenly seemed to have shifted into overdrive. She bent down to pick up the papers, her body tensing as he stooped alongside her to help.

'I can manage,' she said stiffly, not looking at him but following his hands as they swept up the files. He was so close to her that his clean masculine scent filled her nostrils and she had to restrain herself from automatically pulling back. He handed her the files and she carefully stacked them on to her desk, aware of his eyes on her and determined not to let that ruin her composure.

He perched on the edge of her desk and she frowned. What was he doing? She stood behind her desk awkwardly and looked at him.

'I was just on my way out,' she began, and he threw her an ironic, amused smile that made her suspect that he was all too aware of the effect he was having on her.

'How are you enjoying the job so far?' he asked, disregarding her remark totally.

'It's great.'

'I've had some good reports about you.'

'Have you?' She couldn't prevent the smile of pleasure that lit up her face.

'Does that surprise you?' he asked, and she shook her head.

'No.'

'Pretty sure of your abilities, aren't you?' He sounded vaguely amused.

'When it comes to work, yes.'

He looked at her with interest and it struck her again how attractive that dark face was when it did not have the harsh lines of aggression stamped on it.

'That's an odd remark,' he drawled, idly flicking through some of the files. 'Are you not quite so sure of your abilities when it comes to men?' He looked up at her suddenly, right into her eyes, and a tide of pink colour washed her face.

'I really think it's time to go.' She reached out for her bag and his hand shot out to catch her wrist.

'When I say so.'

'Is that an order?'

'Good grief, you make me sound like a Dickensian slave-driver,' he said lazily, but she noticed that he had not denied her question.

She looked down to where his long, lean fingers were coiled around her wrist and her stomach flipped over.

He's bored, she thought. Bored and a little tired, and not averse to having a bit of fun and games at my expense. She tugged her hand and his grip tightened.

'So tell me, why aren't you sure of your abilities when it comes to men?'

'I never said that; you did.'

Her voice sounded steady enough, but the physical contact of his hand on hers had sent her pulses racing.

'You intrigue me,' he said, his grip on her lightening, and he absent-mindedly stroked her wrist with his thumb.

'Do I?' This time her voice was slightly less steady.

'You worked for years in that village library, for instance,' he continued, 'hardly what anyone would call a demanding job, yet you come down here and in no time at all you seem to have mastered all this.'

'I'm sure that must have disappointed you,' Leigh said tightly.

'Are you? Why?'

'Because I got the impression that you didn't expect me to succeed,' she said, still disconcertingly sensitive to the faintly erotic movements of his thumb of her hand. 'You wanted me to work for you so that you could get full value from having been forced to bring us down to

London, but you wouldn't have been too surprised if I had fallen flat on my face.'

He looked at her and his grey eyes glittered with amusement. This, she knew, was Nicholas at his most dangerous—when he was exuding charm without even thinking about it.

She yanked her hand away and began fumbling with her bag.

She wasn't going to let her emotions make a fool of her logic this time. She had learnt a valuable lesson from her last bout of stupidity and it was not one that she was going to forget in a hurry.

'Actually,' he said, loosening his tie, 'I wouldn't have given you the job if I had thought that you were going to fail in it. True, I had no intention of you coming down here and having a free ride, but on the other hand I'm not a masochist. I wouldn't have hired you against my better judgement merely to prove a point.'

'I'm relieved to hear it,' Leigh said, more in control now that there was some distance between them, even if it was only the width of the desk. At least he wasn't touching her. When he was touching her, her brain seemed to seize up.

'And then,' he carried on, still staring at her as if he was trying to work her out, like a perplexing mathematical equation, 'my instincts tell me to distrust you, that you're quite prepared to take advantage of a situation to get what you can. After all, that cottage in Yorkshire needs some major repairs. Yet you don't seem like an out-and-out opportunist.'

He paused and the silence in the room wrapped around them. There was nothing deeply personal in his voice. In fact he spoke with what seemed to be only a mild curiosity, but all the same the atmosphere was disturbingly intimate. Maybe, she decided, it's just my imagination playing tricks on me.

'So can you explain it?' he asked softly.

She looked away, alarmed at the direction this conversation was taking. 'Maybe you should stop trying to work people out as if they were tricky problems,' she said calmly, slinging her bag over her shoulder so that he could be in no doubt that she was going to leave. 'In your profession, I would have thought that the last thing you would have expected of people would have been for them to act according to the laws of logic.'

'On the contrary,' he returned drily, 'you would be surprised how many murders were committed for the most logical of reasons. Money, revenge, passion.'

'Passion isn't logical,' she muttered.

'Maybe you have a point.' He reached over and twisted a strand of hair around his finger, and she froze. 'Or maybe you simply have a barrister's mind—able to twist most things to support an argument.'

'I don't think so.' She wished that he would stop doing what he was doing. She fought down the urge to run— not that her legs felt as though they could take her anywhere. In fact, they felt decidedly shaky.

'So passion isn't logical,' he mused, his grey eyes still fixed on her face, 'in which case, why are you going out with Gerry?'

'I beg your pardon?' His change of topic took her by surprise, and she looked at him wide-eyed.

'Gerry,' he said with a hint of impatience in his voice now. 'Why are you going out with him? I don't believe for a moment that you're passionate about him.'

'What I feel is very personal,' she said, walking towards the door, but before she could flee he had covered the space between them and stood between her and the door, barring her exit.

Was that what all this was about? she wondered. Had it all been leading up to another cross-examination on her motives?

He stuck his hands in his pockets and looked down at her, his mouth twisting cynically.

'That's no answer,' he said.

'It's the only one I'm prepared to give you.'

'Have you slept with him? Does he turn you on?'

She turned white. 'That's none of your business. You might be able to give orders when it comes to work, but what I do in my private life has nothing to do with you.'

'Really?' His voice was light enough, but there was a dangerous glitter in his eyes, which should have warned her, so that she could take the necessary evasive action.

As it was, she was taken completely by surprise when his head swooped down and she felt his lips meet hers in a rough, demanding kiss. Instinctively she tried to draw back, but he reached out with his hand, cupping the nape of her neck so that he could control her movement.

The force of his kiss was such that she could hardly breathe. Everything that was brutal and aggressive was in it, and just when she felt that her anger had reached boiling-point it changed subtly into something altogether more lingering and persuasive.

She felt a nagging ache in her body, which she did her utmost to suppress, but as his mouth found her neck she arched back and groaned slightly.

Everything inside her felt as though it was slowly melting under the impact of her desire.

'You can't possibly feel any passion for Gerry, when you respond to me like this,' he whispered hoarsely into her ear, and immediately she felt her passion begin to ebb.

How could she have allowed herself to get to this point, when cold reason had already shown her the foolishness of responding to him? What was the point of experience if nothing was learnt from it?

'How would you know?' she said unsteadily, stiffening and letting her hands drop to her sides. 'You haven't got some sort of monopoly over arousing women, you know.'

He drew back from her, and all the fierce hunger had left his face.

Right now, though, she could hardly see him. All she wanted to do was to hurt him for being able to manipulate her with such ease. Self-disgust was fanning her anger into an uncontrollable blaze, and she wanted to strike back at him.

'What are you trying to prove anyway?' she shouted. 'That I'm attracted to you? Well, maybe I am, but that's a passing inconvenience.'

'And some women can suffer such passing inconveniences for any number of men,' he bit out grimly. 'Does poor old Gerry think that he's the one and only? Or maybe I was right, and there was no passion there. Maybe, for all your protests, what you have in store for him is just a little more cold-blooded.'

She raised her hand to strike and he caught her wrist. 'Not again, lady,' he snarled. 'If you think . . .'

She wasn't to find out what he thought, because at that moment the door behind him opened and he dropped her hand as though it were red-hot.

Gerry peered at them uncertainly. He had interrupted something, and Leigh could see that he wasn't quite sure what he ought to do.

She forced herself to smile, even though her face felt as if it would crack in the process.

'Gerry,' she ventured in a shaky voice, 'what are you doing here?'

'I phoned the house,' he said, looking at them with the same air of bemusement. 'Sir John said that you were still at work. If I've come at a bad time——'

'No,' she interjected hastily, 'I was just about to leave. We were discussing...work.'

Gerry looked unconvinced, and she could hardly blame him. She knew that her cheeks were burning, and no amount of heated discussion about work could account for their hectic colour.

Nicholas lounged against the wall and surveyed her through narrowed eyes.

There was something threatening about his brooding, watchful silence, and she knew that Gerry sensed it from the darting glances he shot in his direction.

'Why don't we go outside?' she suggested, ignoring Nicholas's presence, annoyed when he clicked his tongue and said under his breath,

'Please, don't let me frighten you away.'

Gerry grinned uncomfortably, and Leigh thought, Poor chap, you probably feel like someone who dives into a swimming-pool only to find that there's a barracuda hovering at the side.

'Actually, I only came to throw you a proposition,' he said. 'Bit of a sudden thing, I know, but I hope that won't be a problem.'

She didn't have to look at Nicholas to feel him listening in the background, and she took Gerry's arm.

'Proposition?' she asked, intrigued. She began walking down the stone steps, helplessly aware that Nicholas was right behind him. She could hardly spin round and tell him to go away, and he knew it.

'My parents,' Gerry explained, 'have suddenly decided to fly to Paris for the weekend, and I thought that we might go to the country house while they're away.' He must have sensed the refusal on the tip of her tongue, because he carried on quickly, 'I've told you so much about it, and you yourself have mentioned that you'd love to visit it...'

'Yes, I know...'

'. . . that I thought that this was the ideal opportunity. We could have the place to ourselves. So what do you say?'

'Yes, what do you say?' she heard Nicholas's voice from behind her, vibrating with mockery. 'I'm all ears.'

She had a childish impulse to turn around and tell him in no uncertain terms where he and his ears could go, but that would probably have thrown Gerry into a state of panic.

But she didn't want to go. Sure, she had told him that she'd love to visit his family house in the country. One day. One day in the hazy future. She never expected that he would take her up on it, and certainly not while his parents were out of the country.

'Well?' he prompted from beside her, his blue eyes looking at her beseechingly.

From behind, she could feel Nicholas's cold grey eyes boring into her back, and on the spur of the moment she said without thinking, 'I'd love to go.' Oh, lord, she thought, as soon as the words were out of her mouth, what have I let myself in for?

Gerry was grinning.

'You would?'

'Why not?' Leigh said unhappily. 'It sounds like fun.'

They stopped outside, the cool evening air whipping around her face, blowing her hair back, and Nicholas leaned towards her until his lips were only inches away from her ear.

'Fun,' he said in a hard voice. 'How touching.' Then he moved away and she watched in dismay as he walked away with that restless, graceful stride.

Gerry cupped her elbow in his hand. 'We'll have a great time,' he promised, and Leigh thought, Will we? Or has my misguided sense of defiance pushed me into something I'll live to regret?

CHAPTER SIX

OVER the next twenty-four hours, Leigh had a good chance to mull over her rash decision to spend the weekend with Gerry.

She thought up what seemed like several hundred excuses which she could use to back out of it, but even to her own ears they all sounded hollow. It would be difficult to sound convincing that something unexpected had cropped up, when only hours before she had informed him that she had no plans for the weekend. Besides, what could crop up with such suddenness? It was hardly as though she had any friends in London, and her life was inconveniently short of sick relatives.

Of course, there was always a sudden bout of flu, but even that lie had its drawbacks. When she last saw him, she was in the pink of health. To be unexpectedly bedridden with flu would try the imagination of even the most gullible.

In the end, she decided that she might as well face the music. She had got herself into the awkward situation, and it would be up to her to handle it as best she could.

She only hoped that there would not be any disastrous confrontational scenes, that Gerry would not see the weekend as an opportunity to exercise a seduction routine.

Oh, lord, she thought, returning from work, for once on the dot of five-thirty, how was it that Nicholas Reynolds had the amazing ability to make her act so out of character? Never in a million years would she have jumped into something unless she was absolutely convinced that it was what she wanted to do.

Freddie's quip, when she told him of her plans, that she was certainly settling down in London quickly, and Sir John's glum disapproval, did nothing at all to ease her frame of mind.

She had a bath and packed her overnight case with all the enthusiasm of someone packing for a stay in hospital.

Gerry had told her that he would fetch her that evening, thankfully after dinner, and she watched the hands on the clock drag by with agonising inevitability.

When Sir John called out that there was someone to see her in the lounge, she glanced at her watch in alarm. It wasn't yet seven o'clock! She groaned inwardly and wondered whether the flu excuse really was as implausible as she thought.

She went downstairs, into the lounge, to find Lady Jessica standing by the mantelpiece, her back to her.

Leigh stopped in surprise. She had not seen the other woman at all over the past couple of weeks. She had almost reached the point of thinking that her antipathy had all been a figment of her imagination, something to do with her nerves after she had just arrived.

Now, staring at that erect back, she had a sinking feeling that she had been right in her first impressions.

'I don't think Nicholas is here,' she said, moving into the room to sit on one of the comfortable sofas, and tucking her feet protectively under her.

Lady Jessica turned around, and gave her a cool, humourless smile. Leigh followed her movements towards the chair facing her, and thought that if there was one thing that she had remembered with faithfulness it was the other woman's striking beauty.

She was impeccably dressed in an off-white silk suit, with a gold-buttoned cardigan in a similar shade.

'Actually,' she said, 'I didn't come to see Nicholas. I came to see you. I thought that we might have a little chat.' She withdrew a cigarette from a silver case and carefully lit it, tilting her head back to exhale a spiral of smoke.

'I don't think Sir John likes smoking in the house,' Leigh said mildly, and Lady Jessica looked at her antagonistically from under her lashes.

'Oh, I don't think that he'd mind *me* smoking. Darling, in case you hadn't realised, I'm practically part of the family!' She gave a low throaty laugh and blew another spiral of smoke towards the ceiling.

'Oh, are you?' Leigh said politely. 'I'm sorry, I hadn't realised. I haven't seen a great deal of you since I arrived.'

That brought a sharp look from Lady Jessica. She flicked her cigarette against a little Wedgwood bowl on the coffee-table in front of her, making no attempt to disguise the acidity on her face.

'Nicholas, poor lamb, has been terribly busy,' she said with a thin smile. 'Normally we can't be separated. But he's been away, and frankly, darling, I've been dreadfully busy myself. Or else I would have come to visit, to see how you were settling in. I know this whole thing must have been such an upheaval for you.'

'I'm settling in just fine,' Leigh insisted, hoping that this conversation was drawing to a conclusion. She glanced at her watch.

'Yes, so I understand.'

There was a heavy silence, while Leigh wrestled with the innuendo implicit in that simple statement. Was there some sort of double meaning there that was above her head? she wondered.

'Yes, the job's very interesting, and I've been trying to see as much of London as I can. The usual tourist sights, you know.' She gave a little laugh, thinking that a pleasant, inoffensive approach might lighten the atmosphere which was hanging over them like a thundercloud.

'Of course,' Lady Jessica said, and Leigh sighed. So much for that line of optimism. She searched around for something inoffensive to say, and was about to comment on the weather, when Lady Jessica broke the silence.

'Actually, I wasn't thinking of the sights. I was thinking more of Gerry. A little bird tells me that you two have been seeing quite a bit of each other.'

Leigh's teeth clamped together. A little bird?

'Really?' she said in a flat voice.

'Oh, don't misunderstand me, darling,' Lady Jessica soothed. 'I think it's marvellous. And such fast work, too. Of course, he's a very eligible bachelor.'

Leigh was beginning to feel faintly homicidal. She clenched her fists at her sides.

'I hate to be rude,' she said with a forced smile, 'but I have quite a bit to do, and...'

Lady Jessica stubbed out the cigarette and gazed abstractedly at her long, pale pink fingernails. 'Just between the two of us, my dear, I'm really rather relieved that you and Gerry are seeing one another.' She gave a little tinkling laugh. 'When you first arrived, I thought that you might have been silly enough to develop a crush on Nicholas, and I know that would have been dreadfully embarrassing for him.'

Leigh felt the blood rush to her hairline.

'Well, you were wrong, weren't you?'

Lady Jessica looked at her, her eyes devoid of warmth, and Leigh felt a shiver run through her.

'I certainly hope so. After all, teenage adulation is such a bore.'

'I wouldn't know. I'm not a teenager,' Leigh retorted.

'I was using the term loosely. Though you do look terribly young.'

That, Leigh thought, made her sound as though she had only just advanced beyond the stage of playing in a sand-pit. She wanted to throw something very heavy in Lady Jessica's direction, but common sense told her that the only way to endure this conversation was to hang on to her temper, even if it was fraying wildly at the edges.

She stood up, placed her hands on her hips and said softly but emphatically, 'I can't imagine what your problem is, Lady Jessica, but, whatever it is, I would appreciate it if you would refrain from taking it out on me. I dislike your tone of voice, and I dislike your attitude. If you can't muster up some semblance of good manners when you address me, then I would rather you didn't address me at all.'

Lady Jessica's mouth dropped open. Her face slowly turned the off-white colour of her silk suit.

'That's very rude!' she spat out, all pretence of politeness gone.

'Which,' Leigh murmured quickly, 'is something you should know all about.' She threw her a freezing, expressionless smile.

This sort of interchange wasn't her style at all, but she had to admit that it felt good. There was definitely something to be said for expressing anger, she thought.

'Now,' she went on, feeling wonderfully in control of the situation, 'was that all? Because, if so, I really have a lot to do...'

Lady Jessica looked at her with cold hostility. 'As a matter of fact, that was all I came to say, and I must say that I wouldn't have bothered if I had had any inkling of the sort of response I would get from you. That sort of rudeness might be acceptable where you come from...'

'Where I come from,' Leigh said, feeling as though she had somehow been relegated to some distant place on another planet, 'there would not be the provocation.'

She stood up and Lady Jessica followed suit, her body stiff as she walked towards the door.

'Just one thing,' she said coolly, turning round to face Leigh, 'I thought you might like to know that we'll be seeing quite a bit of one another over the weekend.'

Leigh stared at her, puzzled. 'I won't be here,' she stated flatly, and received a baring of white teeth.

'I know. You'll be with Gerry at his parents' house. Which is where I'll be. With Nicholas.' There was more than a hint of triumph in her smile now. 'He absolutely insisted that I accompany him. Till tomorrow, then.' And, with that, she swept outside, leaving Leigh rooted to the spot, and feeling very much as though she had won the battle but lost the war.

She had no idea how long she remained standing there, one hand on her hip, the other intermittently brushing back her unruly hair away from her face, but eventually her legs seemed to return to normal, carrying her out of the lounge into the hall, although her mind was still buzzing with unanswered questions.

She was heading up the stairs when the front door opened, and she automatically turned to see Nicholas striding in, divesting himself of his jacket, tugging at his tie until it was unloosened.

'You!' she said, inarticulate with anger.

He looked at her with raised eyebrows. 'Me. Yes. I live here, remember?' He walked towards her and then stopped at the expression on her face. 'I must say, you don't seem in the best of moods.'

Right now, she wanted to inform him, I could quite happily tear you limb from limb and feed you to the tigers in Regent's Park zoo. How dared he cook up some plan with his girlfriend without telling her? Worse, some plan which doubtless had its roots in keeping his eye on her?

'How perceptive,' she hissed, furious that her anger was having no effect on him whatsoever.

'Why don't we have a drink? A whisky perhaps? Alcohol can be very soothing on the nerves.' He took her by the elbow and she snatched her hand away.

'I can think of better things to do with a bottle of whisky than having a drink from it,' she said in a high voice. Like cracking it over that head of yours, she added silently.

'Can you? I have to say you've lost me there.' He propelled her back into the lounge, pushing her into the sofa where she collapsed in an undignified heap.

'So what's this all about?' he asked, pouring himself a drink, after she had refused one through gritted teeth.

'I just had a visit from a certain friend of yours,' she enunciated carefully. Hold the temper in check, she told herself. Histrionics weren't going to win her too many points with this man.

He frowned and sat down heavily next to her. Couldn't he choose another chair? she thought angrily; the room was full of them, for goodness' sake.

'Are you going to tell me who, or do we continue with the guessing game?'

'Your girlfriend.'

'And what did she want?'

'Oh, nothing much. Just to inform me that Gerry and I will be having company for the weekend.'

'So you will,' Nicholas agreed, and Leigh thought, You could at least look guilty.

'And what gives you the right to. . . to barge into my plans without even consulting me?' What she refused to mention was the fact that she was even more annoyed that he had begged his girlfriend to come along, that Lady Jessica had made very sure indeed to tell her that.

'Don't worry, I was going to fill you in as soon as I got home.'

'Well, that sets my mind at rest!'

'Good,' he said and she could have screamed in frustration. It was difficult maintaining her anger when he refused to co-operate.

He removed his tie completely, tossing it on to the coffee-table, and then undid his top buttons so that she could glimpse the bronzed, firm skin with its fine sprinkling of dark hair.

'And do I deserve an explanation?' she asked, averting her eyes from his chest, and trying to concentrate on the matter in hand.

'I got the feeling that you weren't over-keen on the idea of staying at the manor for the weekend with no one but Gerry around.'

'Oh, you did, did you?' She folded her arms, wishing that she could deny what he had said. 'And since when did you become a mind-reader?'

He laughed, and she pursed her lips a little tighter.

'You look like an enraged spinster who has just had her virginity assaulted.' There was definite amusement in his eyes now. It would be so much easier, so much safer, she thought, if he could just be antagonistic all of the time.

'You're insufferable!'

He looked at her thoughtfully. 'You're the first woman to use that adjective on me.'

'You mean Lady Jessica finds you all sweetness and light?'

At the mention of her name, his lips tightened, but he didn't take her up on her observation, instead getting up to pour himself another drink.

'Admit it,' he said, with his back half turned away from her, 'you didn't fancy the thought of the weekend, did you? Just the two of you. Maybe you thought that he might make a pass?'

'Maybe,' Leigh countered, 'he already has.'

Nicholas walked across to her slowly and sat back down, his body only inches away from hers. 'And has he?'

She found herself mesmerised by his grey eyes pierced with specks of green.

'Has he what?' she whispered, unable to look away, aware that she was dangerously close to revealing how attracted she was to him.

'Made a pass at you,' Nicholas rasped, breaking the electrifying current running through them to drink from his glass of whisky.

'That would confirm your impression of me if he had, wouldn't it?' she asked tightly. 'I'm surprised that you thought I didn't want to spend the weekend with him, when you've assumed that I can't wait to take advantage of the poor, unsuspecting soul because he's a meal ticket. Oh, and a quick way to repairing the cottage in Yorkshire.'

'I decided to give you the benefit of the doubt.'

'That was very big of you.'

'Besides,' he relaxed back in the sofa, staring at the ceiling where only a short while before Lady Jessica had been directing her spirals of smoke, 'I need a break.'

Leigh looked at him, noticing for the first time that he really did look very tired. Maybe, she decided, attempting to stifle her feelings of sympathy, it came from burning the candle at both ends. After all, he had not been around much recently. Although... She frowned, remembering what Lady Jessica had told her: that she hadn't seen much of Nicholas recently either.

She had an alarming impulse to reach out and stroke away the lines of weariness on his forehead, which she stifled almost as soon as it surfaced. Her instincts warned her that it was dangerous to let down her defences, for whatever reason.

'Do you?' she asked lightly. 'You disappoint me. I thought you never fell victim to such human things as tiredness.'

He shot her an amused grin and looked at her from under his thick black lashes.

'You thought I ran on batteries, perhaps?' he mocked, but there were no barbed insults in his words. She felt a few more of her defences come tumbling down.

'Long-lasting ones,' she agreed, falling into his mood even though she realised the implicit danger in doing so. 'And you think a weekend in the country is going to revive you? Or do you think that Lady Jessica will do that?'

He gave her a hard, speculative look. 'You talk about her a lot. If I didn't know better, I would be tempted to say that there was a bit of jealousy behind that.'

'Jealousy? Ha!' Leigh shot back in the sofa. Jealous, of Lady Jessica? The idea was ludicrous. 'I just don't like her very much, and the feeling's mutual,' she said stiltedly.

'She invited herself along,' Nicholas said, and she got the feeling that he was talking his thoughts aloud, almost forgetting that she was in the room with him, 'and it might be just the time to get a few things out in the open between us.'

Doesn't he mean out in the bedroom? she thought acidly. She thought of the two of them together and the image was so disturbing that her heart skipped a beat. What's happening here? she asked herself, but she didn't want to pursue that line of thought.

'What fun for you,' she said, getting to her feet. 'I really must go and freshen up before Gerry comes...'

'He's not coming. I'm taking you up tomorrow.'

'You're what?'

'Taking you up tomorrow,' Nicholas repeated.

'Why?'

'Well, you're not attracted to him. And I thought that things might get a bit uncomfortable for you if he took advantage of the situation to make a pass.'

'Or maybe,' Leigh said, breathing heavily, 'you just wanted to keep an eye on me?'

Nicholas shrugged, a dark flush staining his cheeks.

'My knight in shining armour,' she said sarcastically. 'I think I could do with that drink after all.'

'What will it be? Whisky and soda?'

Whisky? She had never tasted the stuff in her life. She nodded and sat back down, feeling thoroughly drained.

I should never have come here, she thought. If I had never come to London, my life would still be trundling along in its own merry way, without all these uninvited complications. She tried to conjure up a picture of her life before Nicholas had barged his way into it, and found that she couldn't. She felt a sudden stab of panic. I don't like the man, at least not very often, and he certainly doesn't like or approve of me, so why then couldn't she imagine life without him?

He handed her her glass and she gulped the contents, feeling the alcohol rush to her head like fire.

'Was that wise?' he asked, inspecting the empty glass.

'You drive me to drink!' she snapped. She raised her eyes to his and then decided that it might be safer not to do that, because his dark, cynical sexiness, combined with the drink, had a disconcertingly destabilising effect on her senses.

In fact, she felt as though she had been dropped into the middle of the ocean, without a clue as to where the shoreline was.

She knew that the best thing she could do was leave the room, but something magnetic in his presence kept her glued to the chair, even though warning bells were clanging noisily in her head.

'If you need a break,' she said, dragging the subject back to safe waters, 'why don't you take a holiday? Go abroad somewhere?'

Nicholas gave the matter some thought. 'I should, I suppose, but work has a habit of building up until the possibility of being away from it for too long is no longer feasible.'

'That sounds rather dreary.'

'And do you think I am?'

'What?'

'Dreary.' He was looking at her with an expression of half-amusement, half-seriousness, and her heart gave another flip.

'Does it matter what I think of you?' she said evasively.

'Have I told you that you have a knack of answering a question with a question? You definitely should be in the legal profession. I can't imagine how you stuck it out working in a library for so long.'

'I like books,' Leigh informed him, looking at him furtively. He really was devastating, she thought, when he was like this—at ease and not subjecting her to the brunt of his aggression. Addictively devastating. She lowered her eyes nervously.

'T-there's something very soothing about being surrounded by books,' she stammered, when he showed no inclination to break the silence between them.

'But not very exciting,' he derided, his sharp eyes taking in the wave of pink that coloured her face.

'I can do without excitement in my life,' Leigh told him firmly.

'That makes you sound like a nun. Besides——' he drained his glass but didn't get up to pour another '—I know you don't mean that. I think you rather like excitement. I think that underneath it all you're as red-hot as that hair of yours.'

Her heart was definitely doing odd things in her chest now and her skin felt as though it was covered with goose-bumps.

There was no answer to what he had said, and she remained silent. He was sitting close to her now, and she edged away, throwing a desperate glance towards the door. He followed the line of her gaze and said softly, 'No, you don't. You're not running away just yet.'

She knew that things were escalating way out of control and she laughed nervously, tempted to try to convince him that running away was the furthest thing from her mind, that all she wanted to do was to revitalise her make-up before Gerry came. Then she remembered that Gerry wasn't coming after all, and it struck her that an evening with an amorous Gerry was far better than an hour in the company of someone whose charm was far more lethal.

Where were Sir John and her brother anyway? No doubt playing chess, a pastime which recently consumed all of their time. They should be here, she thought, rescuing me from this situation.

Nicholas stretched out his arm behind her and she stared fixedly at one of the pictures on the wall.

'However much I suspect your motives,' he said huskily, 'you're still a very tempting woman. Maybe it's because you're so damned full of contradictions.'

Leigh felt herself breathing quickly, like someone short of oxygen. I'll fight this, she thought fiercely, with every inch of my body. He lightly stroked the back of her neck and she pulled away.

'No, you don't,' she whispered, looking at him and then wishing that she hadn't.

His brooding expression was having a drugging effect on her, making her head swim and shifting everything out of focus. This is insane, she thought wildly, re-

member what he is, who he is. Remember your common
sense——— But just now it seemed to have deserted her.

She stared at the sensuous shape of his mouth, holding
her breath as it came nearer, expelling a small moan of
rejection before it found hers. His kiss was soft and assured, teasing her into an unwilling response, then, as
she parted her lips to accommodate it, he kissed her
harder, with more hunger, pressing down against her so
that she was pushed back slightly on the sofa.

Her reason seemed to shut down completely. Her
hands found his black head and her fingers coiled into
his hair, pulling him against her so that their kiss
deepened until she felt as though she was drowning in
it. Under her feverish fingers, she traced the contours
of his powerful shoulders, feeling the rippling of his
muscles under the thin shirt, then she slipped them under
the light material to caress the firm skin.

Nicholas was kissing her urgently, his hand moving to
stroke her breast, then finding the smooth skin of her
stomach under her jumper. Leigh felt as though any
minute she was going to explode. She knew that she had
never experienced this unparallelled sensation of freedom
and excitement, that in some strange way she had almost
been waiting for it ever since he had first touched her.

His hand moved downwards to unzip her trousers and
deftly tug them down her thighs, then slipped underneath her lacy briefs to touch her in places which had
before been uncharted territory.

She could hear him breathing roughly as his body
burnt against hers.

He's going to make love to me, she thought, right here,
in this room, and, as soon as she had silently admitted
that, she suddenly thought, How have I allowed this to
happen? Only minutes previously she had been determined to fight him, to fight herself, with every ounce of
will-power she possessed.

And it wasn't exactly a lifetime ago that she had lectured herself on the necessity of learning a valuable lesson from her response to him the last time he had touched her.

The realisation took place in a split second, and her body immediately went cold. She had been reckless, but there was still time to stop this from happening, and she knew that, however frustrated it might leave her, nothing could be less satisfying than to know that she had let him make love to her because he fancied her. It would be sex without emotion, angry sex because he would have stifled his dislike to satiate his passion.

It was a knowledge that she knew she would never be able to live with.

Her body went limp and she withdrew her hands from where they had been clasped around his neck.

There was nothing so sickening as the sudden death of passion before that passion had had time to reach its climax. She struggled up, pulling her trousers over her legs, zipping herself back into some semblance of propriety, even though her heart was still thumping in her chest.

'What is it?' Nicholas asked, his eyes still drowsy with desire, and she turned away.

'This is disgusting,' she said. 'I can't believe I was crazy enough to let you get this far.'

'Let me get this far?' There was controlled anger in his voice as he straightened to stare down at her. 'Let me get this far? I didn't exactly have to beat back barriers of reluctance!'

'Which is why I said that I must have been crazy!'

She got up and he dragged her back on to the sofa.

'I don't like little teases,' he grated.

'And I don't much care for men who can go to bed with a woman purely through lust! Maybe you think that gold-diggers are fair game. Is that it?' Her anger was as much fuelled by her self-disgust as by him. 'And let's not mention that you seem to have forgotten that you have a girlfriend, and a very possessive one at that. Doesn't that make you think twice before you... you try your hand somewhere else?'

She had rearranged her clothes but she knew that the picture she presented was far from controlled. Her hair was tousled, her lips swollen, and she didn't have to look in a mirror to know that her face was burning with the tell-tale signs of their lovemaking.

Oh, a fine picture you present, she thought, a shining example of a woman in control of her destiny. She wanted to weep.

'Jessica and I aren't married,' he began, raking his fingers through his hair, his voice hard. 'We owe each other nothing.'

This time Leigh did turn to face him, her eyes flashing. 'I see,' she said coldly. 'Well, you have to excuse me if I'm not accustomed to your kind of easy relationships. You'll have to excuse me if I don't agree to take up bed-hopping as a pastime!'

'You don't understand,' he said grimly.

'I understand better than you think! I may be from the back of beyond, but that doesn't mean that I've got cotton wool between my ears! Oh, I understand perfectly well, so please don't patronise me!'

There was a whole lot more she could have said on the subject, but the words remained in her head, swirling in taunting patterns until she wanted to scream.

'I wasn't patronising you...'

'Weren't you? Maybe you were just taking me for a fool, then. A fool who would fall into bed with you because, of course, she has no principles, is only out for what she can get.' Her voice was shaky and hysterical, but she was too angry and humiliated to care. 'I bet it didn't even cross your mind that you wouldn't convince me with those clever, expert hands of yours, that it didn't matter that you disapprove of me, that you're involved with someone else, that...' She ran out of steam and stared at him, her eyes aching from the effort to control her desire to burst into tears.

'I could hit you!' he said savagely.

'And prove what? That you're bigger than me? Stronger than me?'

'Don't tempt me,' he warned thickly, 'and don't try to tell me that you didn't want me as much as I wanted you.'

'Not enough to swallow my dignity!'

'And would you have swallowed it if the stakes were high enough?' he asked in a harsh voice. 'Would you have swallowed it if there was something slightly more solid on the cards? Marriage, for instance?'

There was a long silence and Nicholas looked at her slowly, with dawning comprehension.

'I see. You want me to believe that you're no gold-digger, yet you can't deny what I've just said, can you?' The question hung in the air and remained unanswerable.

Leigh wished to God that she could say something, deny it so that she could erase that scathing look in his eyes, but she couldn't lie. He was right. She had never slept with anyone, not because, as he thought, she was saving herself for the right eligible bachelor, but because to have slept with anyone without the warmth of sharing their love would have been repellant to her.

She got up and walked out of the room, her head held high, and as soon as she was out of sight she ran all the way to her bedroom and lay on the bed, her head thumping, until the tears came.

So this is what pain feels like, she thought miserably. How on earth am I ever going to survive a weekend in his presence?

CHAPTER SEVEN

THE drive up took much longer than Leigh had expected. The roads were busy, and it seemed as if every burst of speed from the powerful car was immediately curtailed by a pile-up somewhere along the motorway.

A couple of times she heard Nicholas swear softly under his breath, clearly irritated by the hold-ups, despite Lady Jessica's persistent efforts at conversation. Poor Lady Jessica. Leigh felt sorry for her. Couldn't she see that trying to drag a verbal response from him was about as successful as trying to get blood from a stone? His replies were uninterested grunts, interspersed with colourful rhetoric on the state of the traffic, which he treated as an aggravating conspiracy designed to get on his nerves.

He was clearly in a foul temper, and making very little effort to hide it.

Maybe, she thought, he was coming down with something. Gastric flu, mumps, the plague, anything that would make him feel as lousy as she did at the moment. Except, it was so much easier to cure a physical ailment. Emotional ones were unfortunately slightly less resistant to antibiotics and few days' bed rest.

And her emotions felt as though they had well and truly been put through the wringer.

The memory of his lovemaking had relentlessly refused to let her go to sleep until the early hours of the morning, and a mixture of her conscience and a sore head were very successfully managing to give this entire stupid trip the proportions of a nightmare.

The only good thing was that he had mentioned nothing of what had happened between them the night before. No sarcastic remarks, no snide insinuations and no taunting *post mortems*, in which she would be certain to emerge the loser.

Not, she thought, that there was any reason to give in to those things. She doubted that she was important enough to warrant more than a shrug of the shoulders as far as he was concerned.

If only she could similarly shrug her shoulders and carry on as though nothing had happened.

God, however could she have let things get so far? She recalled her provocative behaviour with a shudder. She had literally thrown herself, and all caution, to the wind. Who knew what might have happened if she hadn't pulled back? A little voice told her that she knew all right, and she blanked the thought out.

She glanced surreptitiously at him from under her lashes and met his eyes in the rear-view mirror.

'There's really no need to keep checking to see if I'm still here,' she said irritably. 'Believe me, I don't have a suicide wish to let myself out of the car while it's still moving.'

'Thank you for that piece of information,' Nicholas replied drily. 'You can't believe how it sets my mind at rest.'

Lady Jessica glanced sharply at him.

'How much further?' she asked.

Leigh saw the other woman shift slightly, and realised that she was placing her hand on Nicholas's thigh.

Very discreet, she thought. Cars obviously meant far more to Lady Jessica than mere instruments of transport from A to B. Who knew where her hand would be if she weren't lurking in the back?

'Another half-hour,' Nicholas replied briefly, 'thank God.'

'Oh, darling,' Lady Jessica murmured, 'what a bore for you, all this driving, but don't worry, I'll do my best to relax you when we get to Fairbanks.' She laughed seductively and caught Leigh's eyes with an expression of triumph.

Leigh fought back the desire to grit her teeth, and yawned.

'Tired?' she heard Nicholas's deep voice interrupt her thoughts, and she flushed. Did the man miss nothing?

'I'll be glad to stretch my legs,' Leigh said politely. 'Comfortable though your car is, there's a limit to how relaxing any journey can be after a couple of hours.'

'Maybe you've got something on your mind,' he murmured under his breath. 'Tension can manifest itself in so many ways.'

Leigh frowned. She knew that he was referring obliquely to their lovemaking and she was determined not to respond.

'My dear!' Lady Jessica exclaimed, sensing the undercurrent, and not caring for it. 'You obviously haven't much experience of long-distance travel! Have you ever been abroad?'

'Only to France,' Leigh said shortly.

'By plane?'

'Ferry.'

'Oh, well, that's different! Believe me, if you think this is bad, then you ought to try flying to the West Indies! Terribly claustrophobic, even in first class!'

Poor you, Leigh wanted to say, enduring the agonies of aeroplane claustrophobia merely to spend a few weeks lazing on a warm golden beach and sipping cocktails. What torture.

Instead she said drily, 'Thanks. I'll bear that in mind the next time I find myself outside a travel agency, with a few thousand pounds in my hand to throw away.'

She heard Nicholas's deep-throated chuckle and couldn't resist a slight smile of shared amusement.

After twenty minutes of twisting lanes, the car slowly eased through two impressive pillars of stone, up into the open courtyard in front of an awesomely large façade of windows and soft clambering ivy.

They had left the city behind, and were surrounded by open countryside, but even as Leigh stepped out of the car she was vaguely aware that not too far away civilisation was throbbing, waiting greedily to make its way into this carefully preserved piece of uncultivated nature, like a voracious predatory monster.

Still, it felt good to be out of London. Better than she had imagined, even though she had become quite fond of the traffic and the noise. It was easy to become accustomed to the crowded, swift pace of city life until a glimpse of something less hurried showed you that the charms of the countryside weren't so inaccessible after all.

She stretched her arms and legs, feeling them tingle after the constriction of the car.

She reached back for her overnight bag, and Nicholas said to her, 'Leave it. The butler will bring it up for you.'

'Of course. Silly me,' Leigh said with mock self-admonishment. 'When will I ever get used to someone else doing what I'm perfectly capable of doing myself?'

'You saying something?' Nicholas cocked his head thoughtfully.

'Nothing of interest. Just talking to myself. Perhaps I'm going mad.'

Gerry was standing at the door, casually dressed in a pair of shorts adorned with alarmingly bright emblems of tropical birds, and a short-sleeved white shirt. Lady Jessica was talking to him, telling him about the horrendous traffic they had encountered on the journey down, her high voice carrying across the courtyard to where Leigh and Nicholas were still standing.

'Poor darling Nicholas must be absolutely exhausted!' Lady Jessica gave a tinkle of laughter and Leigh looked skywards. She turned to Nicholas as they began walking towards the front door, and asked in a saccharine voice,

'And is poor darling Nicholas absolutely exhausted?'

He looked down at her lazily and drawled, 'No more than you, I expect.' His grey eyes bored into her, challenging her to read something hidden in his words, and she returned his stare with a bland expression.

'Actually, I was a bit tired on the drive up, but I feel quite revived now.' She did too. 'The air smells so much cleaner here.'

'But not as clean as in Yorkshire?'

'Oh, no,' she said gravely, 'there's nothing as fresh or as pure as the air there. On a fine morning, you would swear that there was no such thing as acid rain or the greenhouse effect.'

'You make me wish that I had come back sooner than I did,' Nicholas said softly.

Before she could answer, Lady Jessica stepped resolutely towards them, her dark eyes darting suspiciously, and linked her arm through Nicholas's.

'We're in the green room,' she said coyly to him.

Leigh forced her face to remain expressionless. She reached out to kiss Gerry perfunctorily on the cheek, her mind still busy with images of Nicholas, Lady Jessica and a big brass bed in the middle of a green room. He pulled her towards him and dipped his head slightly, so that Leigh was startled to feel the moistness of his lips against hers. Her instinctive reaction was to pull away, but he pre-empted her resistance by placing his hand gently but firmly behind her neck.

She was aware of Nicholas standing behind her, and on a devilish impulse she responded briefly to Gerry's kiss, before tugging free of his hold.

Let him insinuate and warn, she thought. He can't tell me what to do.

'What a warm welcome!' she said shakily, brushing her hair away from her face. 'Is this how you greet all your female guests?'

He laughed delightedly. 'Only the special ones,' he said in a wicked voice. Leigh smiled. Somehow Gerry could not sound wicked if he tried. He was too nice, too appealingly transparent.

'And there are quite a few of those, aren't there, Gerry?' Nicholas said conversationally.

'Not since I met this stunning creature.' He took her hand and led her inside the house.

Leigh's eyes wandered over the elegant proportions. Since moving to London, her ingenuousness had become slightly tarnished at the edges.

Not so tarnished, though, that she wasn't impressed by the grandeur of her surroundings. Muted, superbly furnished, and if it could be compared to a person it would be to someone wonderfully understated and terribly well bred. She got the feeling that if this house could speak it would be telling Gerry to please change into something more respectable, and could everyone keep their voices lowered?

It was hard to think that Gerry, chatting animatedly at her side, in his gaudy shorts, would one day inherit the place. She had no doubt, though, that by then he would have become far more conservative than he would probably believe possible now.

Nicholas and Lady Jessica were no longer around. They obviously knew the layout of the house quite well, and had vanished to their bedroom. Well, Leigh thought, Lady Jessica had promised to help him to relax, and where better to help someone to relax than in the privacy of the bedroom?

She pushed the thought to one side, and followed Gerry up the stately staircase, channelling her interest into questions about the house and the various portraits on the walls.

The place, she learned, had been handed down through the generations. Along the staircase, in fact, the generations gazed down at them, politely eavesdropping their interchange.

'One day I'll own all this,' Gerry said next to her, with a sweeping, grandiose gesture.

Leigh grinned wryly.

'You'll be the lord of the manor,' she joked. 'Well, you'll have one hell of a cleaning job on your hands. This place must have a thousand rooms.'

'Oh, we have people who come in to clean,' he said.

'Really?' Leigh glanced at him with feigned disbelief. 'I would never have guessed!'

He chuckled and leaned close to her, placing his hand on her shoulder and whispering in her ear, 'Don't you take anything seriously?'

'Of course I do,' she protested, brushing him off uncomfortably.

'Do you take men seriously?'

An image of Nicholas flashed through her head. Tall, dark, cynical, with those eyes that seemed to see everything and give away nothing in return.

'Occasionally,' she laughed uneasily.

'What about me? Do you take me seriously?'

'Well...' she began, hoping that this wasn't leading where she thought it was, but before she could finish her sentence he was holding her possessively by the waist, his blue eyes burning down into hers.

'What about this?' he asked huskily. 'Do you take this seriously?'

Then he kissed her, and this time there was nothing light-hearted about his mouth pressed against hers, his tongue forcing her lips apart, his hands gripping her tightly and making any thought of escape useless.

Leigh fought against an awful, hysterical desire to run away. She liked Gerry, there was something about his boyish nature that appealed to her, but she was not attracted to him, and his searching eager mouth filled her with dismay.

His hands left her waist and travelled the length of her spine, coming to rest under the swell of her breasts.

Her body tensed, and she pushed him back. The movement caught him unawares, and he released her reluctantly.

'Gerry...' she began kindly, feeling very much like someone standing over a child, murmuring soothing words in preparation for a spoonful of spectacularly awful medicine. She stared up at him, searching for the right expression of tact and firmness, and looked past him to the banister. Nicholas looking down at them, one hand thrust into his trouser pocket, in the attitude of a man who had unexpectedly come across a cabaret show and had stayed on to enjoy the spectacle.

Leigh felt her cheeks begin to burn as she was subjected to his scrutiny, then he walked away.

The sudden sight of him had momentarily deprived her of the power of speech and she glared up at the empty space he had left behind, only to find Gerry staring at her curiously.

'You don't have to say anything,' he muttered awkwardly.

'Yes, I do.' Leigh brought her thoughts back to the present, and took his arm lightly. 'But I'd rather not say it here...'

Gerry glanced upstairs shrewdly. 'You mean just in case we're overlooked...again?'

She felt a rush of bright colour fill her face.

'Overlooked . . .?' she said faintly.

'By the big bad wolf.' Gerry's loss of equilibrium was slowly disappearing. He was one of those people who seemed to be programmed to bounce back, whatever the circumstances. He was a sunny-natured individual, and he treated unforeseen upsets in his life as minor inconveniences to be lingered over for a few sad moments before being stepped over in everlasting pursuit of the ray of sunshine just around the corner.

Leigh didn't know whether to feel piqued or relieved at his unspoken acceptance of what she was going to say. Relieved, she decided. Enormously relieved.

'I'm surprised, though,' he was murmuring, as they began heading up. 'Not his style at all to eavesdrop. Funny.'

'Hysterical,' Leigh remarked tonelessly. 'Tell me when I ought to start laughing. Anyway, we really have to get a few things straightened out. Shall we go downstairs somewhere?'

'My bedroom?' Gerry suggested. 'I promise not to come near you.' He looked at her woefully, and added, 'Scout's honour.'

'You were a scout?'

'Dib-dib.' He grinned.

He was true to his word. He listened patiently while Leigh spent ten minutes beating around the bush, finally to tell him more bluntly than she had intended that what she felt for him did not extend beyond friendship.

'Friendship,' Gerry repeated with a resigned grin. 'Trust me to fall in love with a girl who isn't even predictable enough to want me for my money.'

Leigh laughed. I wish you'd tell that to Nicholas Reynolds, she thought.

'I don't suppose all this has anything to do with Nicholas Reynolds, does it?' he asked slyly.

Leigh turned away. It was a stupid idea to have accepted Gerry's proposition to have a serious discussion in his bedroom of all places. It suddenly felt horribly small and claustrophobic, as though the walls were closing in.

It also encouraged strange responses. I mean, she thought, where on earth had Gerry got the idea that Nicholas Reynolds had anything whatsoever to do with her lack of attraction to him? The two didn't follow at all. For a start, couldn't he see that she and Nicholas had nothing in common at all? It was perfectly obvious to her. She might find him attractive, but he had nothing to do with her reactions to anything, for heaven's sake. Nothing. Nothing, nothing, nothing.

She threw Gerry a pitying smile. 'What an idea,' she said, standing up with purpose. 'Nicholas Reynolds happens to be the person I work for...'

'And live with...'

'But not in the way you're implying!' Leigh said hotly.

Gerry shot her a mildly curious look. '"The lady doth protest too much, methinks."'

'A scout and a philosopher as well,' Leigh said, tartly. 'Is there any limit to your talents? Anyway, in case you hadn't noticed, he's more or less engaged to Lady Jessica.'

'I wouldn't go so far as to say that...'

'Well, from the way she clings to him like a limpet, anyone would be forgiven for thinking so.'

'Jealous?'

'Ha! Of course not.' But she didn't care for the way that Gerry was looking at her.

'Time for me to go and change.' She walked across to the door. 'And thanks for being so understanding about everything...' she said over her shoulder.

Gerry's eyes gleamed. 'That's quite all right,' he murmured good-humouredly. 'I think I understand a whole lot more than I did to start with.'

Leigh pretended not to understand him. She rested her hand on the doorknob, and was about to turn it when she heard him say behind her, 'Be careful with Nicholas, though. I wouldn't like to see you hurt.'

Leigh didn't turn around, but his remark had shaken her. He was obviously talking in the dark, guessing at things without realising how uncomfortable his little half-truths were making her feel.

'Don't worry on my account,' she said, staring at the door. 'I can't be hurt by Nicholas Reynolds because I don't feel a thing for him.'

The conversation had given her some food for thought, though, and she spent the remainder of the day carefully monitoring her reactions to Nicholas.

It was difficult. Alarmingly so. They had a light lunch of salad, then went for a walk through the estate, and all the while she talked in a loud, cheerful voice to Gerry, while her eyes slid across with disconcerting regularity, to Nicholas and Lady Jessica, both of whom, she noticed sourly, spent most of the time ahead of them.

She was conscious of each detail of their behaviour, the way Lady Jessica's hand wound around Nicholas's, the way he leant towards her when he spoke, as though every word he uttered was of paramount importance.

The ploy of the inveterate charmer. No wonder he was so successful in his job. He could sell ice to Eskimos.

Was it any wonder that Lady Jessica was hanging on to him for dear life? She had probably already started a collection of aprons and darning kits for when she finally trapped him into marriage. The funny thing was that she was the last person Leigh ever would have imagined to be bowled over by a man. She looked the sort of woman who would be more comfortable in the role of the piper playing the tune. Which only went to show exactly how potent Nicholas's charm was.

By the end of the day, she could not have remembered a word Gerry had said to her, even though she had responded with all the right shows of enthusiasm and interest. She could, however, have recalled with no trouble whatsoever every gesture Nicholas had made towards Lady Jessica, and she would have been able to improvise most of their conversation, because, from what she had seen, it left very little to the imagination.

Lady Jessica, she thought as she prepared for bed later that night, would not have been giggling girlishly if he had been chatting to her about world poverty or the plight of the suffering.

She picked up her book, determined to focus her attention on an altogether more worthwhile subject, only to find that after five minutes the words were blurring over and her thoughts were once again straying to the inevitable.

Two in the morning, she thought with surprise, looking at her watch. A time when most people would be in bed, asleep, instead of lying awake and churning over a guest-list of unwelcome thoughts.

The house was silent. Everyone, she assumed, was fast asleep. Except her. If this continues, she thought, I'll be a raving insomniac within a fortnight.

She tossed aside the book in disgust, and sat up, refusing to spend the next twenty minutes counting sheep.

On the spur of the moment, she slipped on her dressing-gown, and tiptoed downstairs. She was pretty certain that she could have waltzed her way down to Chopin and not succeeded in awakening anyone, but something about the size and silence of the house produced the same effect on her as the village library where she had worked, a thousand years ago.

She felt as though if she made the slightest sound a thin-lipped, cantankerous woman with her hair tightly coiled up would spring from the shadows and proceed to tell her off roundly for disturbing the peace.

So she made her way very quietly downstairs, hesitatingly going in the direction of the kitchen. Once she was safely there, she relaxed and poured herself a glass of milk, and vaguely wondered whether she might be lulled into sleep if she stared hard enough at the pendulum of the clock on the wall. It worked in the movies, didn't it?

If only Nicholas Reynolds would stop invading her mind like a dose of woodworm, crawling in until he was everywhere.

It should, she reflected, be the easiest thing in the world to do. The reasonable, logical side to her said so. If she was attracted to him, then that should be something she could handle with no problem at all, especially when she had the sense to put it all into perspective.

She frowned and wished that reason would put up more of a fight instead of giving in the minute the going got rough.

She had made up her mind to return to her bedroom, and find the prospect of sleep more attractive than she had so far, when a vague noise from somewhere further down towards the right wing of the house caught her attention.

It had not been loud, or even very definite, more a suggestion of a noise, but Leigh felt her hair stand on end.

An open window, she decided. The branch of a tree brushing against the outside wall. Or maybe a fox knocking over something, somewhere outside? All three sounded plausible, but instead of making her way up the staircase she found herself wandering towards the direction of the noise, even though it was really the very last thing she wanted to be doing.

She didn't believe in ghosts, but on the other hand weren't these old places renowned for headless bodies floating about and making nuisances of themselves?

She was about to turn back, when she saw a streak of light emanating from underneath one of the doors, and she breathed a sigh of relief.

Gerry. Of course. He had told her that he kept peculiar hours, often staying up until the early hours of the morning, and only managing to retire to bed when the rest of the world was getting up.

He had said that it was a function of his brilliant mind which restlessly avoided something as mundane as sleep, and she had laughed out loud at that, informing him that it was doubtless a function of his body which had become far too accustomed to a diet of nightclubs and casinos and wild parties that carried on until dawn.

She had every intention of pulling his leg about this. Up at this hour in the morning!

She pushed open the door and froze. It wasn't Gerry in the room at all. It was Nicholas, and he was staring at her as though she were mad.

'Well, well, well,' he said, breaking the silence, and allowing his eyes to roam the length of her scantily clad body.

Leigh pulled her dressing-gown as tightly around her as she could, acutely conscious of the nudity of her legs. How on earth was she to know when she left her bedroom, with nothing on but a tiny nightie and an almost as tiny dressing-gown, that she would end up bumping into the one person in the entire household she didn't want to see? Come to that, the one person in the entire universe she could well do without.

She hovered uncertainly by the door, not knowing whether to dash back up the stairs to the sanctuary of her bedroom, or else to attempt some semblance of sophistication by remaining where she was and meeting his curiously interested gaze with indifference.

'Are you going to linger there by the door for the rest of the morning?' he asked, and Leigh noticed with irritation that even at this hour there was nothing tired or jaded about him. He seemed in total control of the situation, which was more than could be said for her.

'I—I had no idea you were in here,' Leigh stammered, remaining where she was.

'Why should you?'

'I only came down for a glass of milk,' she explained. 'I was on my way back upstairs.'

'And if you had known that I was the one here, that is precisely where you would be now...?'

Leigh shrugged.

'Oh, come in, girl,' he commanded impatiently, 'I'm not going to eat you. I know you probably think me capable of just about anything, but, believe me, I haven't adopted a cannibalistic lifestyle so far.'

'No.' She took a hesitant step forward.

Before she could change her mind, he rose to his feet and shut the door behind her.

It was accomplished so effortlessly that Leigh only realised what had happened when the door was firmly shut and she was facing Nicholas across the room.

And, she thought with dismay, apart from the bedroom, it was unlikely that there was another room in the house as intimate as the one they now found themselves in.

It was small and without the splendour of the remainder of the house. On the contrary, there was something homely and slightly cluttered about this study, with its wood-panelled walls, barely visible behind the shelves of books, most of which were hard-bound and appeared very old. Whose fingers had leafed through those books hundreds of years ago? Were their spirits hovering somewhere now, watching her discomfort?

The Persian rugs which interleaved on the floor were well worn, their faded colours just managing to hark back to a time when the colours were vibrantly exotic. One corner of the room was dominated by a large mahogany bureau, and in the other Nicholas sat comfortably in a tan leather reclining chair, his hands clasped behind his head, his eyes fixed on her with that lazy interest that sent the blood rushing to her head.

Leigh avoided looking at him. She walked across to the bureau and perched precariously on the edge. Why on earth was she here? she wondered. She was getting used to the strange effect he seemed to have on her actions, but this one really took the biscuit. There had to be a thousand more appealing places she could be at three in the morning. Her bed, for one thing. She folded her arms, and adopted a well-this-is-very-interesting-but-I'm-pretty-tired expression on her face.

Nicholas looked not in the slightest sympathetic, and she was beginning to feel acutely conscious of her dress, especially as he was in his trousers and shirt.

'So what,' he drawled, 'brings you down here at this ungodly hour of the morning?'

'Milk.'

'Oh, yes. Milk. What else?'

'I was thirsty. Anyway,' Leigh added, not knowing why she should be the one to do all the answering when his presence in the study was every bit as peculiar as her own, 'I might ask you the same thing. What are you doing here?'

His eyes shifted to the row of books above her head.

'As a matter of fact, I never managed to get to sleep. I gave up pursuing it and came down here instead. To find a book.' He stood up and walked across to the bookshelf, fingering the leather-bound volumes absent-mindedly.

'Well, I won't keep you,' Leigh mumbled. With his back more or less to her, and to the door, it seemed the most opportune moment to beat a hasty and as dignified as possible retreat back to her bedroom.

Before she could slip casually off the bureau, however, he spun around and stared at her with disconcerting thoroughness.

She kept her legs pressed tightly together, wishing desperately that she were at least wearing bedroom slippers, and drew her arms around her body in an embarrassed attempt to ward off his scrutiny.

'You're not.' He laughed shortly. 'I'd be the first to tell you if you were. In fact, it's a refreshing surprise to find someone still up at this hour.'

'Even if it's only me? You do surprise me. Isn't Lady Jessica awake?' she couldn't resist inserting, curiosity getting the better of her resolve to handle the situation with monumental indifference.

'It's possible, I suppose.' He shrugged and sat back down in the leather recliner, rubbing his eyes with his thumbs.

It crossed her mind that for someone who couldn't sleep he looked awfully tired, but there was no way that she was going to mention that. Nevertheless, it softened the barriers which she was trying to erect, and with a sense of shock she realised that what she was feeling towards him was a peculiar type of tenderness.

She looked away in confusion, aware that her hands were trembling. She promptly stuffed them into the pockets of her robe, clenching her fists into tight balls.

'You mean you don't know?'

Nicholas looked at her impatiently. 'You're obsessed with that woman. Does it matter whether she's up or not? I'd still be down here trying to find a book whether she was sound asleep or else doing nude impersonations on top of the bed.'

Leigh stared at him in surprise. The cynicism surprised her because it was so sudden and so out of keeping with his character. Normally he adopted an attitude of amused disdain to anything he found mildly unpleasant.

'Cat got your tongue?' he taunted.

'I...I'm sorry,' Leigh stammered inconsequentially.

'Are you? Whatever for?'

'For...for disturbing you here,' she improvised wildly. 'You look awfully tired,' she blurted out. 'I don't know about you, but I'm going to be exhausted tomorrow. Late nights have a tendency to take their toll the following day. Don't you think? Perhaps not. You must be used to late nights.' I'm rambling, she thought with acute embarrassment. Any minute now I'll be pouring out my life history.

'I am,' he said drily, 'though lately there seem to have been rather a lot of them. But I don't expect you're overly interested in my late nights, are you? Now that we're both here, and the rest of the world is asleep...'

'Or doing nude impersonations on top of the bed.'

'Whatever,' he carried on, but the lines of tension around his mouth had softened. 'Now that we're here, don't you think that there are more riveting things we could discuss?'

He had been tapping on the wooden surface of the desk with his fingers. He now stopped, and fixed her with bright, unflinching eyes.

'Like what?' she muttered into the silence, wishing that he would resume the tapping because that at least had distracted her from the silence in the room.

'Don't you know? Can't you guess?'

'No idea,' Leigh said with a high laugh. 'But if you want me to hazard a guess, then I'd say it had to do with your suspicions of me. Maybe the odd quip about my nocturnal ramblings here having something to do with stealing the family silver?'

'Nothing like that at all. In fact, you're way off target.' He got up and strolled towards her and she looked at him in rising alarm.

'In that case,' she said, backing away, 'I have no idea. I'll go upstairs and sleep on it, and give you my answer tomorrow.'

'Oh, I'll give it to you now.' He raised his arms and propped himself against the door with his palms, trapping her. 'Nothing to do with my suspicions of you. More in the line of carrying on where we left off the other day.'

'Carrying on?' she repeated faintly.

'Oh, yes. We started something that wasn't quite finished. I think it's time we rectified that, don't you?'

CHAPTER EIGHT

FOR a second Leigh's body went as soft and as limp as a rag doll's, then panic jolted her into action.

She pushed against him, giving soft grunts of effort as his arms enfolded her in a rigid hold. She was getting nowhere at all. All that latent strength was holding her tight. It was like trying to beat a retreat through a door of steel.

When Nicholas was obviously tired of her frantic writhing, he pinned both her wrists behind her back in one fierce movement and twisted her body up to face him.

Leigh stopped fighting instantly. It was pointless anyway, and, besides, she had decided to adopt a different ploy completely. She looked up at him and sighed wearily.

'All right,' she said in a tired, defeated voice, 'you win. You've proved that you're stronger than me. Big deal. I can tell you, though, that men who feel that they can win points with a woman by brute force don't impress me at all.'

Nicholas grinned suddenly, his grey eyes glinting down at her. 'Doesn't it? What about a bit of gentleness, then?' He slackened his hold on her, his hand moving to stroke her arm.

She ignored the treacherous urge to be swept away by the hypnotic, rhythmic caress, and pursed her lips tightly together.

Did he think that he could do precisely what he liked, treat her precisely how he wanted, insult her as offhandedly as he cared, and then act as though one smile from him was enough to guarantee immediate forgiveness?

'What about letting me go?' Leigh asked evenly. 'That would impress me most of all.'

'And what about our unfinished business?'

'We don't have any unfinished business between us!' she snapped. 'As far as I'm concerned, that's in the past, and that's exactly where it's going to stay.'

'You mean you don't want me to make love to you? Here? And now? You don't want me to touch you until you can no longer resist? Until neither of us can?'

His words conjured up a powerful throb of desire that left her shaking. She wrenched herself free and moved towards the armchair, afraid that if she didn't she would find that her legs were too wobbly to support her.

'That's right.'

Nicholas walked across to stand in front of her, his hands in his pockets, a half-smile lurking on his lips, and she could have screamed in sheer frustration. The man was so damned self-confident! Years of having his own way with the opposite sex had built up a staggering assurance in his own appeal.

Staggering, Leigh thought frostily, and arrogant. She pulled her robe around her and crossed her legs, and focused her mind on her disastrous behaviour the night before. One mistake like that was marginally excusable. Another would be sheer madness.

'Just because,' she began carefully, 'other women seem to find you irresistible, for reasons I can't begin to fathom, it doesn't mean that I do. I have no intention of jumping in the queue.'

'There's no queue,' he replied mildly, 'and you flatter me. I don't have hordes of screaming women banging on the front door for me. I'm not a pop star. I'm a barrister.'

He sat on the desk and shot her a smug look.

'You've got at least one woman banging on the front door for you,' Leigh said pointedly.

'Jessica.' Nicholas stood up and went across to the window, parting the curtains and peering distractedly outside.

'That's right.'

'We've decided to stop seeing each other for the time being.' His words were clipped, and she couldn't make out whether the decision had been his or his girlfriend's.

Not that it mattered a great deal. Whether he was involved or not with someone else, she thought, made no difference whatsoever. If anything, she would have to be doubly on her guard now, because without the restraining figure of a girlfriend in the background she might find herself all too malleable when it came to his attentions.

She gave him a cool, distant smile.

'And I thought the two of you were so well suited,' she remarked honestly.

'Which just goes to show that how two people blend physically is no indication of how well they blend emotionally.'

He faced her, and his eyes were unsmiling.

Immediately she felt the weight of the silence bearing down on her, making her breath catch in her throat, and fine prickles of awareness spring up on her forearm. She had the most awful feeling that if he so much as feathered her arm with his finger her will-power would desert her, the way it always seemed to whenever he was around.

And she didn't want that to happen. More than anything else she didn't want that to happen.

She glanced across to the door.

'Stop acting like a trapped animal,' he said irritably, following the direction of her gaze. 'I don't want to frighten you.' Then he did what she had been fearing.

He knelt next to her, his head slightly below the level of hers, and touched her on her arm.

She knew instinctively that it was not meant to be erotic in any way. In fact, part of her suspected that he was hardly aware of what he had done. But she felt her body stiffen nevertheless. He felt her response, and the expression in his eyes changed from easygoing friendliness to a searing warmth that sent her pulses racing.

She bared her teeth in what she hoped would pass for a casual but distant smile, and frantically tried to think of something innocuous to say that would break the tense atmosphere between them.

He allowed the silence to stretch between them, until she felt that something would explode, and then he raised his hand to her face and stroked her cheek, his finger tracing the contours of her face.

'No!' she exploded. 'No way!'

'Why not?' His voice was hard and urgent. 'I want you. I've wanted you from the first moment I laid eyes on you. And now there's no longer any Jessica in the background to complicate things.'

'You're missing the point,' Leigh informed him angrily.

'And what exactly is the point?'

'I've already told you, I'm not into bed-hopping.'

'And I'm not into marriage! That doesn't mean that we can't enjoy one another.'

'Don't think that you can talk your way into bed with me!' she broke out vehemently. 'You might have persuaded me to come down to London, but that's as far as it goes! If you and Lady Jessica are finished, and you're looking for a replacement, then you're looking in the wrong place!'

She pushed him, her action catching him unawares, and she took advantage of the fact to run past him towards the door. Now that she was on her feet, she could feel panic clawing at her heels, spurring on her frantic desire to get out of the library before those sensuous grey eyes made her do something she knew she would live to regret.

She pulled open the door, and ran quickly outside, her feet making no sound on the thick carpet. She glanced around and her heart skipped a beat as she saw him following her, his dark, tall body moving like a shot of lightning.

A soft cry escaped her lips and her feet took wings, sending her flying through the darkened corridor into the hallway. Her eyes had adjusted to the darkness in the house, and she skirted around objects, anxiously aware that he was bearing down on her.

Any minute now, and I'll feel his arms around me, she thought desperately. She was a quick runner, had done a lot of track training when she was in school, but even so he was taller than she was, his legs longer, and he was fast.

But she couldn't let him catch her. She knew her weakness for him, and it was that knowledge that made her all the keener to escape him. She shot up the stairs and raced towards her bedroom door, but as she pushed it open she felt him behind her and she gave a groan of alarm and defeat.

She was breathing quickly from the exertion of running, and he was too.

'What are you so scared of?' he asked. Leigh stared at him, wide-eyed, and reached to switch on the light, but he drew her hand away.

'No, leave it off.'

In the shadowy darkness, they looked at each other, and she realised that there was nowhere left to run.

'You still haven't answered my question,' he reminded her softly.

'I'm not scared of anything,' Leigh said, with a stab at bravado. 'But you weren't listening to a thing I was saying...'

'I heard everything you were saying,' he said brusquely, 'and all the things that you weren't.'

'I meant it all, Nicholas. I don't want a relationship with you; I don't care whether or not Lady Jessica has vanished from the scene.'

'That's not what I see in your eyes.'

She turned away and he coiled his fingers into her hair, applying gentle pressure so that she was forced to look at him.

'And when I touch you,' he said softly, 'it's not what your body says.'

'But you don't even like me!' she protested. 'You've been suspicious of me ever since I moved down here!'

'It's part of my nature,' Nicholas said shortly. 'Only a fool lives life on trust.'

'But you can't go through life never trusting anyone.' That sharp edge of panic was fading, and she looked at him with interest.

'I don't normally discuss my private life,' Nicholas began, 'but take it from me that I have had certain experiences that—well, put it this way, that have jaundiced my view of the fair female sex.'

'I know,' Leigh murmured and he shot her a quizzical look. 'Your grandfather told me,' she explained quietly.

'He tells you a lot of things, doesn't he?'

'Please, don't start that again!'

He grinned, and she felt the ground shift ever so slightly beneath her. 'Then you understand,' he said flatly. 'I'm a careful man.'

Leigh gave a little smile. 'For careful one can sometimes read cowardly.'

Nicholas shook his head with a wry expression. 'You're so damned blunt. I can't think of anyone else who would dare apply that adjective to me. Anyway, would you call it cowardly to chase you through this house at four in the morning?'

His voice was husky, and his eyes when she met them were warm and glittering. 'Just stupid,' she said stiltedly.

'Stupid? Stupid, maybe, but certainly not cowardly. Look, I won't pretend that I haven't had my fair share of women, and it's never been my experience to have chased any of them.'

'They drop like ninepins?' Leigh asked drily and he laughed, shrugging his powerful shoulders.

'Something like that.'

'Well, modesty certainly isn't your strong point, is it?'

'No, but I've got quite a few others, if you'd like to find out...'

She was suddenly glad for the darkness in the room, because it concealed the pink tide of colour that flooded her cheeks.

What answer could there possibly be to that blatant invitation? She opened her mouth to say something, anything, when she became aware that they were no longer alone.

The sight of Lady Jessica standing in the open doorway made her blood freeze in her veins. It would have been better if she could have moved a few inches back, out of that suggestive pose with his hands firmly clasped in her hair, but she found that her legs refused to co-operate.

Nicholas slowly turned around and she felt his body stiffen imperceptibly.

'What the hell do you want?' he asked tersely, thrusting his hands into his pockets, but making no move to leave the room.

Lady Jessica wasn't looking at him at all. Her eyes were fixed on Leigh, scathingly assessing the thinly clad body, pinning the blame for their incriminating situation firmly in her corner.

'I heard a noise,' Lady Jessica said in a high-pitched voice. 'I hardly expected to find this!'

'If you go prowling through a house at this hour in the morning, then you should be prepared to find anything,' Nicholas said tersely.

'You two? In each other's arms?' Lady Jessica laughed hysterically. 'What a touching sight.'

'For God's sake,' Nicholas muttered under his breath. He walked towards her and grabbed her by the wrist. 'This is no place for a scene,' he bit out.

Lady Jessica shrieked with laughter, but it was laughter bordering on tears. 'Me? A scene?'

Nicholas turned back to Leigh. 'I'll see you in the morning,' he said abruptly. He pulled Lady Jessica, and she flopped against him, her head resting on his chest, as though she was thoroughly drained.

It was such an unexpected end to the night, or rather morning, that Leigh remained where she was for a few minutes, before moving towards the door and quietly shutting it.

Outside the sky had lightened, and she realised with shock that it would be daylight in a couple of hours, if that. She had slept not a wink all night, and there was no chance that she was going to now. She felt too confused to sleep.

She recalled every word they had spoken, the atmosphere of peculiar companionship that had stretched between them right here in the bedroom only moments before.

What she felt for him wasn't purely physical, as she had tried to convince herself. No, it was more than that. Leigh drifted across to the large bed, and watched the sky through the open curtains. Disparate thoughts were gradually beginning to knit together. Little things that she had shoved to the back of her mind were slotting into place.

She realised that whenever she was in his company she felt more alive, even when they were arguing, even when she felt so angry at something that he had said that she wished she could lift the nearest heavy object and hurl it at him. He ignited little sparks inside her, and when those sparks weren't ignited she was like a hollow shell, talking, walking, carrying out her daily chores but without momentum. It dawned on her that even when she was thinking of him she was fired with some strange inner flame.

I've fallen in love with him, she thought in bitter awareness. After all the hours spent reasoning why he was the very last person in the world I should even like, I've fallen in love with him.

No wonder she had become addicted to following his every movement greedily, surreptitiously, delighting in all those idiosyncrasies which she had been so determined to hate.

She tossed restlessly on the bed, unable to get to sleep, but unable to focus on anything other than him. She wondered what was going on in the green room between him and Lady Jessica. He had told her that their relationship had been broken off, but now a thousand sneaking suspicions began to filter through her mind.

Leigh busily worked on every connotation of what had happened between them, trying to figure out when exactly she had stepped beyond the line of physical attraction to that of emotional need.

Not, she thought wearily, that it mattered. Nothing had changed, only her awareness of the situation, and it would have been much better if that had remained the same. It was true what they said about there being bliss in ignorance.

She was just beginning to drift into a light doze when there was a sharp rap on the bedroom door, and Leigh sat up abruptly. Her first thought was that it was Nicholas, and she buried herself into the bedclothes before shakily telling him to enter.

It was even more important now that she would not give in to him, because she stood to lose far more than she had ever thought possible. So she adopted her very primmest look, pursed her lips tightly together, and mentally rehearsed her speech about feeling deeply exhausted.

The door was pushed open, but it wasn't Nicholas at all. It was Lady Jessica, and Leigh felt a sudden stab of apprehension. 'I think you've come to the wrong room,' she said in what should have been a haughty voice, but what sounded like an uncoordinated squeak.

Lady Jessica closed the door quietly behind her and pulled the chair from the dressing-table to the side of the bed. From this angle, Leigh felt her initial stab of apprehension mushroom into something decidedly more foreboding.

The small bedside lamp was switched on, and it threw a pattern of light and shade across Lady Jessica's face, turning it into an angular and threatening mask.

Leigh looked around for some object of self-defence. Who could tell what was going to ensue? she thought. One minute, the semblance of a rational conversation, the next minute a frenzied attack. She laughed nervously to herself and decided that too little sleep was beginning to have a disastrous effect on her imagination.

Nevertheless, she continued to eye Lady Jessica with wary discomfort, and she found herself unconsciously edging towards the side of the bed until she could go no further unless it was on to the floor.

'I think it's time we had a chat,' Lady Jessica said in an icy voice.

Leigh licked her lips and ventured a polite smile. 'Couldn't we leave it until the morning?'

'It is morning.'

'Oh, yes,' Leigh murmured. 'What I meant was, couldn't we leave it until another morning...?'

'I don't think so. There is, after all, no time like the present.'

Personally, Leigh could think of a thousand times much better than the present, but she kept her observation to herself. It didn't take the IQ of a genius to realise that Lady Jessica was in no mood for weak attempts at humour.

'I suppose you think you're clever,' Lady Jessica said in a hard voice, 'to have wheedled your way into the Reynolds's house, pretending to be the hard-done-by little country girl who couldn't tell a fish-knife from a chain-saw. You must have thought it would be a cinch to get in touch with the wealthy friends the minute your grandfather died, and wangle an invitation to London. After all, who could resist all that clear-skinned, freckled, rustic stupidity? Certainly not Nicholas. As I told you once before, he always was a push-over when it came to down and outs, especially pretty little ones like you. Though what he sees in those cowlike, innocent charms, God only knows.' She paused to take a deep breath.

Leigh stared at her in amazement. She had been prepared for vitriol, but the depth of the other woman's hatred left her open-mouthed. She was almost too surprised to feel anger.

'Well, you misjudged him.' Lady Jessica's eyes narrowed, giving her a malevolent appearance. 'He knows you for what you are—a pitifully obvious little fortune-seeker.'

Lady Jessica gave a harsh, abrupt laugh, then she bent forward, and Leigh was deeply grateful that she had put as much distance between them as she had been able.

That glare at close quarters would have been enough to rival anything Medusa had to offer.

Her eyes widened in alarm, but when she began to speak she found that nothing emerged except for an indecipherable grunt. Her normally quick-witted brain had failed her, and the repertoire of biting repartees revolving in her head were staying there, leaving Lady Jessica a wide-open, silent field in which to parade her venom.

'Don't think that I'm so stupid as not to have seen your pitiful attempts to attract Nicholas's attention. You're attracted to him, aren't you?'

Lady Jessica noticed the mounting red colour, and her lips tightened.

'I see you can't deny a word I'm saying,' she said in low, sharp tones, 'and I suppose if the little scene I broke up here a few minutes ago was anything to go by you must be in your element, but I wouldn't start counting chickens as yet...'

There was a leaden pause as Lady Jessica fastened her eyes triumphantly on Leigh. She looked ghastly in the early grey morning light creeping into the room, her features distorted by a deep, burning resentment.

'I'm sorry,' Leigh ventured, 'that you had to witness it...'

Her voice trailed off, as she realised that the first intelligible sounds to emanate from her mouth only appeared to confirm everything that Lady Jessica had just accused her of.

'What I mean...' she began.

'I know precisely what you mean,' Lady Jessica replied, her words razor-sharp, 'but believe me when I tell you that I'm not at all sorry that I was fortunate enough to walk in and disturb your little game of seduction...'

'Game of seduction...?' Of all the nerve, Leigh thought, her anger finally beginning to find an outlet.

Seduction! Her! Anyone would think that she had been caught red-handed parading in black stockings and suspenders and a come-hither smile on her face.

True, their interlocked bodies did not exactly spell out an accidental encounter, but it made her furious to know that she was being cast into the role of the seductress.

She spluttered angrily and was about to defend herself when she was cut off by Lady Jessica, in full flow and determined, Leigh thought, not to allow any attempts at interruption to her wrath.

'You heard me,' she snapped, throwing her head back, her dark eyes flashing with hatred. 'You must have thought it the climax to your little act. Did you stay up until you realised that Nicholas wasn't coming up to bed, then go down to the study to confront him? I supposed you played on the fact that, even if he suspected your motives, he was still a man, and most men find a willing female very difficult to reject. Which is why you ended up here in the bedroom.'

Leigh would have loved to answer the questions with a few well-phrased replies.

'Well,' Lady Jessica swept on, disregarding Leigh's high-pitched response, 'it's a good thing, as I said, that I walked in on the two of you. God knows what would have happened if I hadn't. All I know is that Nicholas would have lived to regret it. We both know what sort of plans you've been harbouring, but you had better exclude Nicholas from them . . .'

'Plans?' Leigh managed to find her voice, albeit several decibels higher than normal. 'Harbouring? What do you think I am?' A stupid question since she knew full well what Lady Jessica was getting at. Had the two of them discussed her? Laughed at her? It very much sounded so.

'A conniving little vamp, my dear.'

Leigh stared at her, aghast. Any minute now, she thought, two sharp fangs would appear and Lady Jessica would transform into a vampire. Clad in her black satin robe, with her dark features, she definitely radiated something not quite human.

'Well, you're wrong!' Leigh succeeded in finding her tongue, which she had begun to think was stuck to the roof of her mouth. 'Not that I care what you believe.' She looked at Lady Jessica witheringly, and couldn't resist adding, 'Though I'm surprised at your reaction. From what I gathered, you and Nicholas have split up.'

There, she had said it. It was a bit below the belt, but then all of Lady Jessica's remarks had been as well, and there was no reason why she should have the monopoly on snideness.

There was an electric silence. Leigh could almost hear the sun rising outside. She looked pointedly at her bedside clock, yawned so widely that she heard her jaws click, and hoped that Lady Jessica would seize it as an opportune moment to leave the bedroom.

'What an illicit thrill that must have given you,' Lady Jessica went on spitefully, ignoring Leigh's carefully directed hints, 'listening to details of what was no business of yours!' Two red spots had appeared on her cheeks, and Leigh could almost feel sorry for her. After all, hadn't they, ironically, something in common?

They had both made the mistake of loving the same man, when common sense should have warned them to run a mile the minute they set eyes on him.

'What did he tell you?' The tell-tale flushes of pain had vanished, and the alabaster-white skin was cold and hard.

'Oh, nothing, really,' Leigh prevaricated awkwardly, regretting having ever said anything.

'Did he tell you that we had agreed to split up?' Lady Jessica looked at her searchingly, and Leigh nodded.

Even in her confused frame of mind, those words had a familiar ring to them.

Lady Jessica gave a triumphant snigger.

'And do you know why he phrased it like that?'

'I have no idea,' Leigh said shortly, with the instinctive feeling that she was about to hear something unpleasant, 'and I don't particularly want to know. I haven't slept for more hours than I care to count, I'm tired, and I don't much want to sit here and play twenty questions with you.'

It was the most lucid retort she had managed since Lady Jessica's unexpected appearance in her room, and it made her feel much better. After all, why should she lie in this strait-jacketed position in her bed and listen to someone whose only motive in talking to her was inspired by hatred? All she wanted to do was bury herself under the blankets and quietly nurse her misery.

'I didn't realise that we were playing a game,' Lady Jessica replied smoothly, an icy smile cracking the marble-white veneer of her skin. 'I thought we were having an adult conversation about something that matters to both of us...'

Really? Leigh thought, feeling anything but adult.

'It may matter to you, but it doesn't to me,' she lied, lowering her eyes to her entwined fingers.

'Oh, I think it does,' Lady Jessica intoned relentlessly. 'You're after Nicholas. Sure, you entertained Gerry for a while as a possible catch, but it's Nicholas you really want to get your tenacious claws into. It's as obvious as the nose on my face. Do you really think I haven't noticed the way you follow him around with your eyes? It's laughable. We both think so.' She paused for breath, and Leigh looked at her in horror.

She simply wanted the earth to open up and swallow her up because she had never felt so humiliated in her entire life. Follow him around with her eyes? she thought.

Had she been so obvious? She squirmed with mortification at the thought.

She only hoped that he had not guessed at the horrendous truth that she was in love with him. Almost better to be treated as a gold-digger than scorned as a gullible idiot.

Her face was white, but her voice remained calm and flat when she replied to Lady Jessica, 'You must be crazy. I never wanted to come down here. Nicholas persuaded me that it would do Freddie good to get out of Yorkshire for a while. As far as I'm concerned, I'd return to my home village tomorrow·if it weren't for my brother. As for being after Nicholas...' The words almost stuck in her throat. 'Ha! Your imagination's been running away with you!'

'I'm glad to hear it,' Lady Jessica commented, holding up her elegant hands and pretending to inspect the long, polished fingernails. She rested them languidly on her lap and crossed her legs. 'I wouldn't want to see you hurt, after all.'

Sure, Leigh thought acidly. And pigs fly. 'Fine,' she said. 'Now are you finished?'

'Yes.' Lady Jessica stood up and flicked imaginary flecks of dust from her robe. 'Oh, just one last thing. I never got around to explaining why Nicholas told you that we had agreed to split up. I mean, don't you think that's a very odd way of putting it?'

'No.'

'Well, the reason he said that is because I finished with him, and not the other way around. I hate to point out the obvious, but the only reason he indulged you when you made a pass at him was because he was probably depressed.' She smiled a crocodile smile. 'Maybe he thought that you were better than nothing?'

She spun around, leaving Leigh staring open-mouthed at her, and walked out of the room, quietly closing the door behind her.

Better than nothing, Leigh thought viciously. She snatched one of the pillows from the bed and hurled it at the shut door, narrowly missing some porcelain ornaments on the nearby shelf.

She might as well face it; there was no way that she was going to get any sleep at all. She glared at the light streaming through the window and turned on her side. She wanted to die. How could she have let that odious woman come into her bedroom and spend half an hour insulting her? It was the first time she had ever allowed anyone to even think of insulting her without vigorously defending herself.

But Lady Jessica had caught her unawares, and by the time she had gathered her wits together it was too late. Insinuations had been made, accusations slyly targeted, and, even though she knew that most of it had been founded on lies, Leigh still found the distasteful remarks turning over repeatedly in her head. Niggling, poisonous little insects that left her stomach churning over uncomfortably.

She tried desperately to think back to Nicholas and what had happened between them in the study, but the details became elusive. All she could remember with any clarity was the strength of her response to him, the fierce need she had felt to get away before she allowed him to show her just how vulnerable she really was. And that was just about the last thing she wanted to remember.

Lady Jessica's words were vividly clear in her mind, though. At a push she could recall them word for word, and every word had been like a drop of acid.

Had he really made a pass at her on the rebound? Had he wanted someone else to be there in the study with him? Someone who had decided to end the affair?

She would have laughed aloud at the idea of Lady Jessica's being the one to give Nicholas the push, when her every move seemed designed to attract his attention, but if he had been the one to finish things, then why didn't he come right out and say so? Was it because, she thought bitterly, gold-diggers didn't deserve explanations?

She finally fell asleep at the unearthly hour of six o'clock in the morning.

She was oblivious of all the early morning sounds, oblivious to everything until almost eleven o'clock, when she emerged downstairs, feeling not in the slightest refreshed for her sleep, to find that they were going to leave much sooner than expected.

'Jessica's ill, apparently,' Gerry confided mournfully to her, as he sat opposite her at the dining-room table, watching her consume a cup of black coffee and three croissants.

'Is she?' Leigh asked uninterestedly. Let's hope, she wanted to add, it involves a few years' bed rest.

'Looks awful, and she's absolutely insisted on being driven back to London as soon as possible. In fact, she would have left already, but Nicholas waited for you.'

Leigh chewed unhurriedly on her croissant.

'He needn't have. I could have caught the train back.'

'I could have dropped you, although it would have been difficult. I've got to be here tonight.' He beamed cheerfully at her, and Leigh attempted to beam cheerfully back.

She would have lingered endlessly over her breakfast, feeling not in the least guilty that Lady Jessica was in a hurry to get back, but Nicholas appeared in the doorway with a look on his face that insisted she hurry up.

Leigh looked at him, drinking in his dangerous good looks, wishing she could detach herself from the emotions pounding through her. After everything Lady

Jessica had said, after everything that she herself had painstakingly reasoned, she still wanted him, still felt that odd quiver of excitement when she saw him, or heard his voice, or even knew that he was near by somewhere. Where was that celebrated Yorkshire pride now when she needed it most?

She finished eating quickly, packed in even more record time, and almost before she knew it she was in the car, in the back seat, trying to ignore the painful knot in her heart.

CHAPTER NINE

THE drive back shot past. One minute they were surrounded by open fields, and the next they were edging back into London, manoeuvring through the treacle-slow traffic and listening to the radio inform them of enough tailbacks to put one off cars for life.

Leigh suddenly had an overwhelming desire to get away, to get back to the simplicity of life in Yorkshire, where the days drifted happily into each other and she still had control over her emotions.

She looked at the dark head in front, sneaking a glance in the rear-view mirror to see the handsome features frowning with concentration as he tried to edge into the flow of traffic.

Then she looked at Lady Jessica's sharp profile, the mouth drawn into a tight line. She had spoken very little on the drive back. What had she been thinking? Was she regretting her decision to finish with Nicholas? Had she decided to re-cultivate their relationship now that she thought there was a rival on the scene? Maybe she had been thinking of something more basic, like a thousand and one ways to murder a rival without being caught.

Humour, she thought dejectedly, was a poor defence against being in love. How could someone have such power to crush all her carefully fabricated defences with just one gesture, as if they were a stack of cards? There should be a law against that.

What would her grandfather have said about it all? He had brought her up to be totally self-reliant, had drummed into her the importance of being independent. She thought with bitter irony how little it had taken for her to realise that her independence was so much hot air.

She only noticed that they had arrived when the car pulled up outside the house, and Nicholas informed her that he would let her out before dropping Lady Jessica back.

'Of course,' Leigh said tonelessly. Why not? Maybe he sensed a big reconciliation scene on the cards.

'Leave the bags,' he instructed. 'I'll bring them in when I get back.'

'Fine,' she murmured, 'there's no rush.'

He looked as though he was about to get out of the car to open her door, and to forestall him Leigh jumped out, slamming the door behind her, and walked up to the house, not bothering to glance in Lady Jessica's direction. She had had enough acidity to last a lifetime. She could do without another dose.

From behind her, she heard the car swish back down to the road, and she was quite proud of the fact that she steadfastly resisted the urge to spin around and see whether Lady Jessica's forgiving arm had slid up behind Nicholas's head.

When Freddie opened the door, she swept past him in a fit of anger, not seeing him at all, and not aware of his presence until he called out after her in surprise. She slowed down, took a few deep breaths, counted to ten, and turned to face him, a large, tinny smile plastered across her face.

All she wanted to do was get into a hot bath, shut her eyes and pretend that she was several million miles away, but she thought guiltily that she had barely seen Freddie over the past few days, and had not the faintest idea what he had been up to.

And, she thought guiltily, she was supposed to be here in London for his benefit.

She cast one lingering look in the direction of the staircase and followed him into the sitting-room.

For once, his usual boisterousness was missing, even though the tousled blond hair falling across his eyes still managed to conjure up the image of someone dying to play a practical joke.

Through the blur of her own chaotic emotions, Leigh listened and responded to what he was saying, hardly taking it in, until he hesitatingly informed her that he was thinking of doing his apprenticeship in the little village close to their home in Yorkshire.

Leigh sat up at once.

'But I thought you liked it here!'

'I do,' Freddie hedged, 'but I miss home, and, besides, we can't leave it unattended forever.'

'I meant to get back,' Leigh interjected defensively, 'soon. As soon as you were settled.'

'I've been settled for a while,' Freddie replied mildly. 'I mean, the apprenticeship's been fixed up for some time. I've really only been hanging around here because of Sir John.'

'Sir John?' Leigh asked, at a loss.

Freddie coughed and reddened with embarrassment. 'Sure; the old man's become accustomed to having me around.'

'Has he?' This was news to Leigh, although, casting her mind back, she did seem to recall that they had been getting along exceptionally well. In fact, only a few days ago, she had been delighted when she had met Sir John coming back from a morning in London, on his own, the first in a long, long while. She had not associated his sudden independence with her brother, but of course it all now fitted together. It was just that she had been too wrapped up in her own affairs to notice what had

been going on around her. Now Freddie wanted to go
back home and it was like a bolt from the blue.

How could she leave London? She had become accustomed to it, for heaven's sake! She fidgeted restlessly,
half listening for the front door, and thinking that of
course the best solution to all her problems had been
solved by her brother. If she returned to Yorkshire, then
she would free herself from the bog she seemed to be
stuck in, and gradually things would return to normal.

She stood up and said firmly, 'Good.'

'Good?' Freddie looked at her, bewildered. 'What's
good? Are you feeling all right, sis?'

'Of course I'm feeling all right. Why shouldn't I be?'
She waited for him to answer and when her question was
met with a bemused shrug of the shoulders she repeated
stoutly, 'I've never felt better, in fact. And as for your
decision to return back home, good idea. That's what I
meant by good. We've both had enough of London, and
I agree with you—it's high time we went back to where
we belonged.'

'Sure. One thing, though—Sir John's coming as well.'

'As well?' Leigh repeated faintly. 'Sir John?'

'Do you mind?' He looked anxiously at her. 'We've
been discussing it for the past couple of weeks, and, well,
he hates it here. Says it's like a morgue.'

'A morgue?' Things were happening very quickly here.
Too quickly. She felt disorientated.

Freddie nodded. 'Haven't you noticed anything?' he
asked querulously.

Not much, she thought with a guilty pang. 'It's just
such a surprise. Where will he live in Yorkshire?' Stupid
question.

'With us. The old man needs someone to look after
him. You don't mind, do you? I kind of miss Yorkshire,
to tell you the truth. Don't you?'

'Sure,' she lied. Miss Yorkshire? Never. Not when the alternative was living in the presence of an arrogant, in-furiating, insulting man.

'You're right, of course,' she found her voice. 'We can't simply vanish from the cottage forever. Heaven only knows what state it'll be in when we return.' She tried to think of the actuality of getting on the train and never seeing Nicholas Reynolds again, and felt a quiver in the region of her stomach.

Of course, Sir John coming with them, delightful though the prospect was, was just another nail in her coffin. More scope for accusations of gold-digging. She was realistic enough to realise that wild horses wouldn't be able to stop him from renovating the cottage. He would look at all the repair work that needed doing, and he would be insulted if she denied him the chance to do it.

Freddie's decision sealed her fate. And wasn't it for the best? What did she expect her future to hold? A lifetime of moping about behind a man who wanted her body but considered her beneath him when it came to involvement?

A stint in hell would be better.

'We can't live off charity forever,' she continued more confidently, pushing aside images of the vacuum awaiting her in Yorkshire. 'I mean, I'm earning good money now, even if it is through Nicholas. I've got enough ex-perience now to look for a better job. Yes, the time is just right for going home.'

Home. Didn't quite have the same ring about it as when she had just left it behind. Then, it represented everything she had ever known, all her little joys and disappointments, memories of her grandfather. Now, it would always remind her of her grandfather, but she felt as though reality, her life force, was where she was now.

'Are you sure you don't mind about Sir John coming?' Freddie repeated, standing up. She firmly pushed him back into his chair.

'I told you. It's settled. When were you two thinking of leaving?'

'Next weekend, we thought, but it all depended on you...'

'Suits me. Anyway, Freddie, darling, do you mind if I go upstairs and have a bath? I mean, I know I haven't seen much of you recently, but maybe we can plan on being together a bit more next week. We can enjoy the last week here together, and then good riddance!'

She glared at him, because mysteriously his puzzled, boyish face had metamorphosed into the hard, arrogantly chiselled features of Nicholas, and left the room.

She spent the next thirty minutes luxuriating in the bath and trying to persuade herself that leaving London was precisely what she wanted to do. Deep down. She held up one soapy hand and ticked off the reasons why. Firstly, there would be no Lady Jessica in Yorkshire. She would be free of the uncomfortable jealousy that swamped her every time she was in the other woman's presence. Secondly, the air was cleaner up north, and she would be able to cycle everywhere in the open air instead of rushing around by Underground—like a mole. Thirdly, Sir John would give Freddie the stability he had so missed when their grandfather died. He would be no problem now. His life, if not hers, had some direction.

And of course, overwhelmingly, she would be free of Nicholas. She would no longer have to confront that hard, sexy face on a daily basis. She would no longer find herself dwelling on his attractiveness, both physically and intellectually, and then be forced to spend the next few hours reminding herself that it was all a useless game.

No. There would just be the three of them.

It was a wonderful prospect, she thought glumly, wrapping the large, fluffy towel around her. She frowned miserably and decided that she couldn't be happier, since everything was going to be sorted out.

She was so busy re-convincing herself that things couldn't be better that she almost missed the dark figure sitting comfortably on the chair in the corner of the room. She was about to throw aside her towel, when her eyes caught his reflection in the dressing-table mirror, and she spun around as though suddenly given a huge electric shock.

'What the hell are you doing here?' Her voice was trembling and she clutched the towel to her, backing away from him, even though he had made no effort to come towards her.

Nicholas smiled, but it did not quite manage to reach his eyes. 'Waiting for you.'

'Why?' she bit out, then continued, not giving him the opportunity to reply, 'And you could have waited somewhere else!'

'I'm sorry,' he said, folding his arms across his chest in the attitude of someone who had just arrived and was settling in for an indefinite stay, 'the door was unlocked.'

'That's no excuse!' Leigh replied in a high, shaky voice. 'Banks are open during the day—that doesn't mean you can feel free to have a quick nap in one if it takes your fancy!'

'That's an obscure metaphor,' he said calmly, and she had the sudden feeling that whereas he was a little uncertain when she had first emerged from the bathroom he was now, as usual, totally in control. Her display of anger had placed her in the vulnerable position, and her lack of clothes didn't much help either.

'You know what I mean,' she answered, trying to inject a similar note of calm into her voice, 'and, besides, what are you doing back here so soon?'

'What do you mean?'

'I thought that you were dropping Lady Jessica off.'

'I was and I did.'

He looked at her, and she could have kicked herself for indulging that particular piece of curiosity. She had thought that they would have had an explosive reconciliation, slept together for the rest of the day, and he had seen right through her remark to what had been going on in her head.

She was seething with jealousy, like some silly sixteen-year-old whose best friend had stolen her boyfriend—and he knew it.

She turned away with a sour taste in her mouth.

'I came here to find out what the hell's going on with you,' he said, leaning forward so that his elbows were resting on his knees. 'I mean, I thought we were getting along so well at Gerry's place, however inappropriate it was, and then this morning you were like a block of ice, for no apparent reason.'

Getting along well? Leigh thought fiercely. No apparent reason? The words reverberated in her head until she felt giddy.

'No, please don't change,' he said urgently, as she made a move towards the wardrobe. 'I want to finish what we started a long time ago. As I said, there are things to be settled between us. I want to make you mine.'

He had risen from the chair and Leigh watched in horror as he walked towards her. Didn't he understand that what they had started could never be finished? Couldn't he get that through that thick skull of his? She loved and wanted this man more than she would ever have dreamed possible, but she had finally come to her senses and seen that she could never accept the crumbs that he had to offer.

She opened the door to the wardrobe and snatched at the first dress that came to hand, one of her old cotton affairs that she had almost forgotten existed.

His hand reached out and grasped her by the wrist.

'Well?' he asked, his voice quick and breathless. Close to, she could see the naked passion in his eyes, a burning light that pierced through her and began kindling her own inner heat. It frightened her because she realised beyond the shadow of a doubt that his hold on her would never be relinquished merely because she might decide to put some distance between them.

The thought filled her with anger. Why should she be the one to suffer? Her going back to Yorkshire damn well wasn't going to have any lasting effect on him. He would shrug his shoulders and get back to work. She, on the other hand, would probably spend the rest of her days pining for him, a man who didn't deserve two minutes of her thoughts!

It just wasn't fair! She stared into the inviting depths of his eyes with frozen antagonism.

'What's changed,' she said with careful self-control, 'is me. So I admit that I was attracted to you, but I was a fool to ever think that sleeping with you would have been fulfilling for me. I very nearly made a mistake once.'

'Are you saying that you're no longer attracted to me?' Nicholas asked, watching her face with savage intensity. 'That you've changed into someone who wouldn't give me the time of day?'

'That's exactly what I'm saying.'

'I don't believe you.'

'Fine. Don't.' She leant over to retrieve her dress from the bed and felt his hands on her shoulders. 'Get your hands off me!' she very nearly shouted, straightening up quickly. Her still damp hair clung around her neck like seaweed and underneath the flimsy barrier of the towel she could feel her heart thumping in her chest.

'Kiss me and then talk to me about change.' He half closed his eyes and bent slightly towards her. 'I've been thinking of you all day, dammit. I haven't been able to get you out of my mind. You can't just tell me that you want nothing to do with me. I won't allow it.'

'You won't allow it?'

The audacity of the man staggered her. She would have walked away from him, her head held high, if it weren't for the vice-like grip of his fingers on her shoulder-blades.

'How can you expect me to?' he moaned huskily, one hand moving to warm the back of her neck. 'You're in my thoughts all the time. Every time I close my eyes, every time I blink, I have visions of your naked body in front of me and it's been driving me mad!'

The warmth of his breath was doing funny things to her, making her perspectives shift in a most alarming way. She stood back firmly, pulling away from him, and blinked.

She felt like saying, Well, how do you think I've been feeling, when I'm not only attracted to you, but in love with you as well? Instead, she said tonelessly, 'You think the worst of me, and yet you still want me. Too bad.'

He gave a short laugh, and ran his fingers frustratedly through his tangled black hair. His eyes ran the length of her body. His movement then was so swift that Leigh didn't know what was going to happen until he pulled her back to him and tugged her head back, his fingers clasped hard in the damp, knotty mass of her hair.

'Look,' he said with a dark flush, 'I was wrong about you, all right? Dammit,' he muttered forcefully, 'how can you tell me that you want me out of your life? You're still as attracted to me now as you ever were; we know that. And I'm going to prove it to you.' His lips ground down savagely over hers, prising her mouth into submission. Leigh struggled and gave a small, defeated moan as her body went limp against his.

It was useless fighting with him. He was bigger and stronger than she was. It would only take him one flick of the wrist to prove that. But that didn't mean she had to give in to him.

She felt his mouth roving feverishly over his, his tongue licking against hers, and, with a superhuman effort of will-power, she refused to respond, even though her body seemed to be slowly melting under his caresses. She continued to clutch at her towel, her body clenching when she felt his hand grasp her naked bottom, stroking the smooth skin upwards to the small of her back.

Every touch was agonising. She tried desperately to think of something terribly dull and boring, but nothing could distract her from his urgent siege on her senses.

Nevertheless her rigid body must have finally cut through to him, because his caresses gradually lost their fervour, and he stepped away from her in bafflement. 'What are you trying to prove?' he demanded harshly, turning away from her and walking towards the window, his hands clenched in his pockets.

'I'm trying to prove that what I told you last night, what I'm telling you now, wasn't said for fun. I meant every word of it. I don't want an affair with you, I don't care if you realise now that I wasn't after your money. It doesn't matter. I just want you to leave me alone. Is that so difficult for you to understand?'

Nicholas shook his head and sighed impatiently.

'I don't believe you.' But his voice bore the slightest inflexion of uncertainty.

'You don't have a choice,' Leigh informed him.

He didn't. He stared at her and she could see the realisation of what she was saying beginning to sink in.

He wouldn't rush across to her, she thought, because she didn't mean that much to him. He had wanted her, but he wasn't going to fight to have her. He certainly wasn't going to declare undying love and ask for marriage, which, deep down, was what she knew she wanted so very badly. Why should he? Lady Jessica was just around the corner, and Leigh was certain that the other woman would have him back if he asked. And he wouldn't have to promise her anything at all, because, from what she had seen over the past few weeks, Lady Jessica was quite happy to sleep with him whether marriage was on the cards or not.

She had probably broken things off through a fit of pique, and pique was the simplest of emotions to vanish with a touch of adroit persuasion.

'I intend leaving here pretty soon,' Leigh said with a hint of defiance, wanting to spark a reaction out of him.

'When?' He looked vaguely surprised, but not taken aback.

'Probably this coming weekend,' she replied in a dull voice. Inside she was screaming for him to go. She hated what he could do to her, and she hated the fact that, however much she would have liked it, she had no power over him at all. 'And you might as well know that your grandfather has decided to come with us. Freddie and me. We'll both be out of this house and out of your hair for good. And, before you start voicing your suspicions, no, I'm not after your grandfather's money. Although, quite frankly, I don't give a damn what you think.'

'I see,' he said coolly, walking across to the door, his eyes glancing uninterestedly at her. 'I'll know now to make the necessary arrangements for someone to take over from you at work.'

'It shouldn't be a problem.'

'No. The money's good enough.'

Leigh mumbled her agreement. Her heart was pounding painfully in her chest, and yet here she was, having this trivial conversation with the man who had single-handedly managed to wreck her life.

She watched as he turned the doorknob and quietly let himself out of her room, then she ran to the door, locked it, and sat heavily on the bed. Her body was still burning from the need to have him near her. Maybe, she thought bitterly, she should have a cold shower. Perhaps that was how she was destined to spend the rest of her days—having cold showers—because even the thought of him was enough to make her tremble with want.

The prospect didn't thrill her. She had a vivid picture of a shrew-faced, middle-aged lady who spent half her time under a running cold shower, and the other half glaring jealously at couples walking hand in hand. It would all be his fault.

The ache was still gnawing away at her the following morning when she arrived at the office. She had braced herself to see Nicholas, to act as though nothing had happened between them because that was how he himself would act, but in fact there was no need. He was out of the office, and, she was told, he would be for the rest of the week.

'He's had to go down to Devon to see some people relevant to one of his cases,' Richard, the older of the clerks, informed her.

'Well,' Dave corrected, 'he didn't have to. He decided to at the last minute.'

Leigh could feel disappointment flooding into her. So he had decided to make sure that he didn't set eyes on her again before she left. She wouldn't even have the small leeway of a week to take her final sidelong, hungry glances at him, to fill her head with images of him because they would have to last her the rest of her life.

She worked in a daze for the balance of the day, hardly noticing what was going on around her. It helped that they were very busy, so her silence didn't arouse curiosity. It was merely taken for granted that she was too engrossed in trying to keep up with her workload to have much time to chat.

And she did her utmost to encourage the impression. She spent the day frowning with her most businesslike and rushed-off-her-feet frown, and generally did her best to look harassed and overworked. Richard and Dave left her to herself, and underneath the veneer she indulged in a never-ending flow of thoughts and regrets.

What if her grandfather had not died? What if that wretched brother of hers had not become entangled with the law? What if their solicitor had not seen fit to contact Sir John without first informing her? Most of all, what if she had been sensible enough to listen to her head and not her heart?

By the time she left the office, she felt as exhausted as she had spent the day trying to look. She stopped off to buy a newspaper, and tried to plan as many things as she possibly could for the evening. Freddie and Sir John would be in, of course, playing their game of chess, which seemed to have developed into a soothing habit for the both of them. If she didn't do something, anything, there would be just too much time on her hands for her to think about Nicholas.

She dawdled on the way back to the house, stopping to browse in some of the shops on the high street, anything to kill time and have the comfort of strangers around her. She almost indulged in a mad impulse to buy something thoroughly expensive and totally unnecessary, but who knew what her source of income would be over the next few weeks? She had no intention of relying on Sir John to keep her and Freddie in board until she found work.

Expensive impulse-buys, she consoled herself, were the sign of a weak person. Instead, she bought a bar of chocolate and derived the same wicked feeling from eating it very slowly on the walk back to the house.

Now that the prospect of never seeing Nicholas again had become a reality, everything she did seemed to be in slow motion. Time dragged in a way which she would not have thought believable, and years seemed to have elapsed before dinner was finally over and she had retired early to bed with her newspaper.

She glanced through the front pages, her eyes skimming over the inevitable stories of other people's terrible misfortunes. Then she came to the page that she disliked reading, but always read anyway. The gossip page. A handful of insights into the lives of the rich and famous.

She saw it almost immediately. It screamed at her from the very centre of the page. It had been given the prime spot and the journalist had focused salaciously on every delicious detail of one of London's most eligible bachelor's forthcoming marriage to one of London's most eligible débutantes. The gilded couple. Nicholas Reynolds and Lady Jessica.

Leigh felt her face blanch and she had apparently developed rigor mortis in her hands, because they could neither turn the page, nor could they release their vice-like grip on the paper. She read the article, which was brimming over with jocular chumminess, very quickly at first, then more slowly. Then she re-read it, at a snail's pace, the implication of what was written in front of her finally sinking in.

Marriage. Lady Jessica and Nicholas. She had been wrong about Lady Jessica. She had mistakenly thought that the glamorous débutante had been willing to have an affair with Nicholas, no strings attached, but obviously she had been holding out for something more. Perhaps that had been the source of their argument? The ultimate choice between marriage or nothing? Well, she had got it.

She had trapped the biggest fish in the sea, according to the article. There was a picture of her, smiling, her head thrown back for the camera. At just the right angle, of course.

Nicholas might have deferred the inevitable marriage to have a quick fling with her, but she had killed that. Her revelation about Sir John's decision to live with them had no doubt made him rethink his admission that perhaps she was not the gold-digger he had assumed.

Leigh crumpled the paper ruthlessly and flung it across the room, then she jumped out of the bed and began throwing her clothes into her suitcase.

Everything was carelessly tossed in. Cosmetics, shampoo, the few expensive items of clothing she had invested in—it was all jumbled together in a chaotic mass.

She didn't care. Nothing mattered any longer, except the need to get away from London, and to hell with what Nicholas or anybody else thought.

It was not quite nine o'clock. She would be able to make it back to the village by the early hours of the morning. It all made perfect sense to her that she get out of the house with the utmost speed. The newspaper article was stifling her. At least in Yorkshire she might be able to breathe without this awful feeling that she was going to choke.

She was genuinely baffled at Freddie and Sir John's alarm at her course of action.

She announced that she was about to leave, just as Freddie was about to make his chess move, and she almost laughed at the expression of dumbfounded amazement on his face. It was so funny, but at the back of her mind she knew that if she burst out laughing it would dissolve at some point to tears, and those she could never explain.

'Do you know what time it is, sis?' he asked helplessly, reading the stubborn expression on her face.

'Of course I do,' Leigh snapped, smiling apologetically at Sir John, and glaring at her brother. 'By the way, Sir John, I'm so glad you'll be staying with us. The Yorkshire air will do you a world of good.' God, she thought, I must sound crazy.

'I thought we'd agreed on next weekend,' he commented, glancing covertly at Sir John.

'You had,' Leigh informed him, picking up her holdall and hoping it would indicate that the conversation was drawing to a close. She turned to Sir John, whose mild expression made her feel far more sheepish than Freddie's outright curiosity, and thanked him sincerely for having put them up.

'It'll be great seeing you again. What a good idea that I'm going up now so that I can get the cottage straight.' I really do sound crazy, she thought again.

Sir John frowned. 'Your sudden departure hasn't got anything to do with my grandson, has it?' he asked shrewdly.

'Nicholas? Oh, no. No, no. Of course not.' She gave a little choking laugh. 'What a thought.' If I don't leave now, she thought, I'll definitely be in a strait-jacket by tomorrow morning, the way I'm acting.

Sir John looked worried. She hoped he wouldn't be worried enough to get in touch with Nicholas. Freddie looked as though she'd taken leave of her senses.

She gave a last warm, firm smile that made her jaws ache, and left the house with Freddie scampering behind her like a puppy, using every argument conceivable to try to get her to stick it out for the remaining week. She walked very quickly, at least grateful for his help with the bags, and dodged all of his outright questions.

'Be good,' she said when they reached the Underground, and kissed him impetuously on the cheek.

'Phone and let me know when I can come to meet you at the station.' Then, inconsequentially, she added, 'Isn't life a barrel of laughs?'

'What?' Freddie asked, bewildered.

'Oh, nothing.'

When she finally made it to the platform, where she was informed by an impersonal voice on a Tannoy system that the train she wanted to catch was running an hour and a half late, it was as uncrowded as she had expected.

She sat on her case and mournfully watched the assortment of people who would be her companions for the next few hours. None looked remotely interesting, but then to be fair, she thought, she probably looked as uninteresting to them as they did to her—a waif-like figure in a faded cotton dress, a baggy cardigan, and long red hair trailing down her back.

She hugged her knees to her chest, resting her chin on them fighting the stab of unhappiness at the back of her eyes. More than anything, she didn't want to cry, because that would only re-confirm her hurt. She wanted to be as bright as she could, then maybe she would begin to believe that things weren't as dreadful as they felt.

She heard footsteps approaching her, but she didn't raise her head. Whatever he or she wanted couldn't possibly be worth looking up for.

Then she heard him speak, that arresting voice that she had been so struck by the very first time they had met. Her pulses began to race, and she felt suddenly dizzy as she raised her eyes to meet Nicholas's.

CHAPTER TEN

LEIGH'S mouth had gone dry. She stared up at him for what seemed like eternity, her body rigid with shock. He was looking back down at her, his only sign of vulnerability the fact that he looked dishevelled, as if he had spent days without sleep. Otherwise, his eyes betrayed no expression.

'What are you doing here?' Leigh asked in a strangled voice, remembering why she was here in the first place, sitting on her suitcase in an uncomfortable train station. She was cold, sleepy and aching, and it was all his fault. How dared he just stand there and look at her with those flint-grey eyes as if the whole situation weren't absurdly unnatural?

He didn't answer. Instead he held out his hand to her. Could he really think that she was going to be fool enough to take it, and let him lead her away like some ten-year-old miscreant being taken back home? She looked at it with distaste, and looked away.

'Come on,' Nicholas said tightly, 'this is no place to hold a conversation.'

'I agree,' Leigh replied, 'which is why I don't intend budging from this spot; so, you see, it's been a complete waste of your time coming here.' Freddie must have told him where she was. She was going to kill that brother of hers if it was the last thing she did.

He squatted down beside her, so that his face was only inches away from her own. Up close, he looked even more tired, and Leigh was tempted to make some wisecrack about his appearance and burning the candle at both ends, but she had a feeling that she would promptly burst into tears if she tried to be humorous. And he wasn't looking terribly light-hearted either. There were lines around his eyes which she had never noticed before, and his face had a greyish look about it that made her wonder exactly what nature of candle he had been burning at both ends.

She looked away, angry with her thoughts.

'Don't be obstinate, Leigh,' he said roughly.

'I'm not being obstinate.'

'No? Prove it. Stand up and come with me to where we can talk in some privacy. I think——'

'I don't care what you think!' Out of the corner of her eye, she could see a few of the people on the platform looking at her curiously, and she realised that she and Nicholas were providing a welcome cabaret for them on a platform where absolutely nothing else of any interest was happening. The interested eyes turned away when they saw that she was glaring at them, but she knew that the minute her attention had refocused on Nicholas they would swivel back in their direction, eager to pick up from where they had left off.

'Everyone's staring at us,' Leigh whispered furiously.

Nicholas shrugged. 'Let everyone stare. It really doesn't bother me.'

'Well, it bothers me!'

'Then let's get out of here. There's a coffee-shop just around the corner that stays open till midnight.'

'I'm not thirsty. And I already told you: I'm not going anywhere with you.' She tried to look steadily at him, but the directness of his gaze unsettled her, and she focused her attention on her fingers instead, twining them nervously together.

Her head was thumping and she wished that he would just go away. Why had he come to see her anyway? Did he feel sorry for her? Responsible? She was visited by the unwelcome memory of Lady Jessica telling her how kind he always was to the underdog.

Or maybe, she thought darkly, he had come here to find out exactly what her intentions were now that Sir John was coming up to Yorkshire with them. More accusations now that he had had time to think it all over.

'Fine,' he said briefly, settling into a more comfortable position beside her. 'We'll talk here, but don't start complaining because people are taking an interest in what's going on. You know how intrigued bystanders get at the slightest whiff of excitement.'

'I don't want to talk to you!' Leigh almost shouted, and she heard a voice say from somewhere behind her,

'Oh, go on, give the guy a break.'

'You see what I mean,' she hissed. 'Just go away. I want to be alone.'

'Why?'

'Because . . .' she spluttered, trying to find a calm, logical answer to his question.

'Don't you mean you want to run away?' he asked mildly, though his eyes were deadly serious. 'She wants to run away from me!' he said to their general audience in a loud, clear voice, and a woman answered with a laugh,

'Let her. Then you and I can get together.'

Leigh was horrified. A handful of people had grouped closer to them, and, with Nicholas's remark seen as an invitation to drop all pretence of uninterest, they were openly waiting for the next instalment in the drama.

She refused to look at them. She refused to look at him, though she could see obliquely that he was grinning.

She might have guessed that he would enjoy playing to an audience. Wasn't that his job, after all?

She knew that her cheeks were flaming with embarrassment, and that she had somehow managed to be tossed into the awkward position of either staying put, and having her entire personal life played out to an eager crowd, or else acquiesce to him, and let him lead her to the coffee-bar. Pride kept her rooted to the spot. If people had nothing better to do than eavesdrop on their conversation, then let them.

All the same, she leaned forward slightly so that her long hair draped across her face, blocking out the unwelcome sight of their faces.

'Is that coffee-bar beginning to look more attractive?' Nicholas asked in a low voice.

'No!' Leigh snapped. 'I don't want to go anywhere with you!'

'Good for you!' a woman encouraged. 'We don't need men. They're nothing but a bunch of chauvinistic pigs anyway!'

'Not a feminist!' a man's voice yelled out, and there was a ripple of glee as general debate on the subject broke out, with the feminist firmly holding her ground, and managing to recruit a couple of unlikely giggling teenage girls to her cause.

Leigh and Nicholas were temporarily forgotten. The whole thing, she thought bitterly, would have been amusing, if she weren't at the epicentre of it. She had never before witnessed a crowd of British strangers throwing themselves into an argument with quite such a lack of restraint.

'No one will miss you if you go now,' she told Nicholas coldly.

'You will.'

'I beg your pardon?' Leigh's eyes angrily clashed with his. 'How dare you? You must be the most arrogant, egotistic, conceited man I've ever met in my entire life!'

'And you must be the most stubborn, pig-headed woman I've ever come across!' he countermanded.

'Fine! We're agreed, then; we dislike each other!'

'I never said that. I happen to quite like stubborn, pig-headed women.'

Leigh could feel something inside of her melting at the intimate timbre in his voice, and she reminded herself that the man was no more than a bastard, and an engaged one at that.

'Well, I don't happen to like arrogant, conceited men.'

'Arrogant, egotistic, conceited men. You forgot the egotistic.'

'And it isn't a big game either!' she yelled, close to tears, forgetting their eager eavesdroppers.

'You don't have to tell me. It's deadly serious, isn't it?' He looked at her, and she felt herself struggling against the desire to yield to whatever he wanted. He was hypnotic. He had the amazing power to drag all her well-meaning intentions into a whirlpool of sensation over which she had no control.

But she wasn't going to allow it. She had too much to lose.

The hubbub around them was beginning to die down, and the clutch of bystanders were politely but persistently trying, once more, to edge into their conversation.

'We haven't reached a decision on anything,' Nicholas informed them, and there was a disappointed sigh from the crowd.

'You'll never sort anything out on a station platform,' an elderly man with a briefcase pointed out. 'It's much too unromantic.'

'And when,' his female companion retorted, 'have you ever been into romance?'

'There's nothing romantic about this!' Leigh felt constrained to inform them, much as she disliked their predatory interest in what was none of their business. She hoped that the firmness of her tone would disperse them, but if anything it seemed to encourage their participation in what they obviously considered a juicy, human drama.

And the train wasn't due for at least another fifteen minutes! She rested her head in her hands and groaned inwardly. How was she going to last out? She felt as though she was being battered on all sides. As though Nicholas had somehow managed to woo the crowd on to his side, and she was being cast into the role of the *belle dame sans merci*.

'Why don't you want to talk to me?' he persisted, making no effort to lower his voice, encouraging their faithful following to sympathise with him.

'I don't think we have anything to say to each other,' Leigh responded.

'I think we have a great deal.'

'Of course,' she said sarcastically, 'like what you're doing here when you're engaged to be married to someone else?'

'You're engaged,' the feminist exclaimed in a horrified voice, 'to someone else? That's dreadful!' She looked around dramatically, relishing her unexpected limelight. 'Typical. Men. They're all the same. Wasn't that what I was saying a moment ago? They don't care how they hurt women, just as long as they get what they want.'

'Ssh,' a muscled youth with tattoos on his arms signalled. 'The man might have something to say for himself.'

'This is none of your business!' Leigh protested limply. The comment was received with icy disapproval. I give up, she thought. This is a ridiculous situation, and I just can't cope any longer. She would have left the station, if she could have done so without having to face Nicholas outside.

She glanced at his cynical, handsome face and a flicker of amusement crossed his features.

It suddenly struck her that he was playing the situation with all the skill of a musician on his instrument. His involvement of the crowd had gone a long way to dissipating her anger with him. It was what he had wanted, and he had succeeded in achieving it. The opportunist.

She smiled weakly at him, and someone said, 'I think we're getting somewhere here.'

'But what about the fiancée?' another voice chipped in.

There was a roar as the train pulled laboriously into the station, screeching to a halt, and disgorging its passengers with bored indifference.

The crowd was clearly dejected at its arrival. They picked up their briefcases and carrier bags, and Leigh was swept under a flurry of well-intentioned advice.

'Have the coffee with him!'

'Go back home. You're better off without types like that. Chauvinist.'

'You could do a lot worse, dear.'

'Well?' Nicholas said, not trying to detain her. 'Your train's here. Do I get you to listen to what I have to say, or are you too much of a coward for that?'

Leigh raised her eyes to his, and he brushed her hair away from her face. His fingers against her skin were warm, and she wanted to swoon at the feel of them.

'I...' she began, then he was kissing her, his mouth moving over her parted lips, raising a loud cheer from their audience, who were hanging out of the windows, reluctant to bid goodbye to such a riveting drama.

'It's love!' someone cried out, and he unpinned the carnation in his buttonhole and threw it at them just as the train pulled out of the station.

It landed on Leigh's shoulder. She stood up, desperately. The train. It was pulling away. Her lifeline to recovery was slowly leaving the station, and she wasn't on it.

'I must get on,' she wailed.

Without the comfort of strangers around, the platform was disquietingly empty, devoid of all human life apart from a couple of stragglers and a guard.

And them. Leigh looked surreptitiously at Nicholas and felt a tingle of alarm shoot through her.

'That was the last train tonight,' he said finally.

'I know that! You don't have to state the obvious!' She got up and struggled with her various bits of luggage, grudgingly letting him relieve her of some of her burden.

'Coffee?' he asked.

She didn't answer. She wanted to hit him, stamp her feet and burst into tears all at the same time. She had fought so hard to maintain self-control a while back. Now here she was, going with him to that wretched café he had mentioned. He had got what he wanted. As usual. And he still hadn't answered her question about Lady Jessica.

She wished that she didn't care so much about it, but she did. She could feel the jealousy and anger eating away at her, tenaciously chipping at her equilibrium and destroying that peace of mind she so desperately wanted to establish.

She followed him out of the station, which was strangely quiet at that late hour of the night, and into the nearest taxi.

'I thought it was just around the corner,' she said dully, not much caring where he was taking her.

'Depends which corner you're talking about.'

He gave the taxi driver an address in Knightsbridge, and they sat in silence through the journey. Leigh didn't even look in his direction. She didn't need her heart to start playing its usual tricks on her whenever she saw his face.

And he seemed absorbed in his own thoughts as well. His forehead was creased by a small frown, and she hoped that whatever was bothering him would keep him awake for nights.

When the taxi dropped them off, Nicholas instructed the driver to take the luggage back to the house. She didn't have the heart to protest, not that there would have been much point. She could hardly return to the station and wait there for the next train out.

The coffee-shop turned out to be the lounge in a very expensive hotel. All subdued and quiet. She remembered the elderly man's comment about the station platform being too unromantic for a conversation, and she desperately wished that she were back there now. Discomfort was a great aid to anger.

Here it would be altogether too easy to relax. She settled back into the comfortable chair, and realised that she was hungry.

He must have read her mind, because he ordered coffee and sandwiches, informing her that he was starving. 'You must be too,' he commented, and she shrugged, managing nevertheless to make her way very rapidly through three ham and cheese toasted sandwiches, and a slab of chocolate cake. It settled happily on her stomach, and relaxed her even further.

This was one of the reasons that she so loved him, she realised. He always seemed so tuned in to her needs, even the elementary ones. Was it like this with Lady Jessica? A knife twisted somewhere inside her, and she bit back the tears.

'Tell me why you ran away,' he said casually, as though their broken conversation at the station had only been a few seconds prior. 'Was it because of what you read in the newspaper?'

'Newspaper?' Leigh tried to look blank, and succeeded only in looking guilty.

'Hmm. The one I found lying on your bed, open at the page announcing my imminent marriage to one Lady Jessica Thompson.'

Leigh didn't comment. To deny having seen the article would have been transparently obvious. On the other hand, to admit that she had read it, in fact had devoured it word for word and very slowly, would have been tantamount to an expression of how she felt about him.

She stuck her finger on to a cake crumb and licked it, resolutely ignoring him.

'Well?' he persisted.

'All right,' Leigh conceded irritably. 'I read the article, and it came as a bit of a surprise, but that's not why I left.'

'Ah.' Nicholas sat back, his arms folded across his chest, and stared at her expectantly.

'I left because...' She thought quickly. 'Because there's a problem at the house.' There. It sounded plausible. She knew it did, because the smug expression had been wiped off his face. He looked taken aback. Leigh smiled politely at him and licked another cake crumb from her finger.

'What kind of problem?' he asked, frowning.

This was beginning to get ridiculous. She might have guessed that one small white lie only led to much bigger, more elaborate and not quite so white lies.

'Water.'

'Water?'

'Yes. One of the pipes burst.'

'In that case,' Nicholas pointed out, hanging on to the subject like a dog with a pet bone, 'why didn't you say that from the start? Why all the coyness? Were you hoping that I would adopt a caveman approach to get you out of that station?'

'Certainly not!' Leigh said loudly, noting with relief that this time there were no spectators within earshot.

'Because it certainly worked, didn't it?'

'I didn't want to be dragged here!' she denied hotly. Somewhere inside her a little voice told her that this was precisely what she had wanted. She had wanted to prolong the time she had in his company, and she was glad that she was sitting here, because at least she was invigorated instead of pathetically miserable.

'I think you did,' Nicholas said roughly, 'and, more than that, I don't believe a damn word about any burst pipes. You would have mentioned it to Freddie before you left, and he would have told me immediately. In any case, even if all the pipes had packed it in, why race off in the dead of night? You wouldn't have been able to do a thing, and common sense would have told you to wait until morning. So, you see, I'm not buying your little story, so try again.'

She didn't. The burst pipe was the best she could come up with under duress, and it was miserably lacking in credibility. She fidgeted with her coffee-cup, then stuck her hands under her thighs and sat on them, because it was the only way she could manage to keep them still.

'So we're back to that article,' he commented. The exhaustion seemed to have vanished from his face now that he had thrown her on the defensive. Barrister's tactics again, she thought sourly.

'I had no idea you were going to marry Lady Jessica,' she finally admitted, knowing that he would not let the matter rest until he had dragged the truth out of her.

'I wasn't.'

'Then what made you change your mind?' She could not conceal the edge of bitterness in her voice, but she couldn't care because in a few hours' time she would be on that train out of London and out of his life. For reasons best known to himself, he had succeeded in detaining her, but it was only temporary.

She had not realised it, but she had leaned forward and was sitting on the edge of the chair, her hands gripping the sides, as she waited for his answer.

'I didn't.'

Leigh laughed acidly. 'You're telling me that the newspapers got it all wrong? Right down to the picture of a gleeful Lady Jessica? I've heard of the Press fabricating stories, but not to that extent!'

'Maybe I should make myself clear,' Nicholas interjected.

'Suit yourself.'

'And stop pretending to be so damned indifferent,' he said through gritted teeth.

'Fine. I'm listening.'

'The story wasn't altogether untrue. They quoted Jessica absolutely correctly when they printed that our marriage had been announced.'

Leigh felt as though she had dropped a thousand feet, leaving her stomach somewhere very far behind. Her knuckles were white from gripping the chair. She was sure that her nails had pierced the thick velvety material, but for the life of her she couldn't relax her hold. His words, reverberating in her head, would not allow it.

'But,' he continued, then paused as though he wanted to marshal his words very carefully, 'what they didn't know was that any wedding announcement was news to me.'

'You're saying that she lied?' Leigh whispered. Some of the colour that had drained away from her face was returning. 'But why?'

'I suppose I was largely to blame,' he said heavily. 'I assumed things that weren't so. For instance, I assumed that we viewed the relationship from the same perspective. Something to be enjoyed, but with no pretence of permanency. She certainly seemed to accept it willingly on those terms.'

'Or maybe,' Leigh said slowly, 'she didn't. But you just never read the signals correctly.'

'You could be right,' Nicholas conceded after a while. 'I can be remarkably thick in some areas.' He looked directly at her and she felt a strange fluttering in her stomach. The charm of the devil, she thought. Was that why he had rushed back to London? Because he wanted to make sure that she didn't believe what had been printed, since he still wanted to get her into his bed? She knew that it was an unfair assumption, but it was so much easier to fight him when she had some form of weapon on her side.

'I don't know when,' he said soberly, 'her light-hearted fling with me developed into something more... obsessional. I only know that when we broke off our relationship she was inflamed.'

'You broke it off, didn't you?'

Nicholas nodded and asked, 'Why?'

'Because she told me a completely different story. She said that it had been her decision, and left me in no doubt that she could have you running back to her at the snap of her fingers.'

'Really?'

Leigh nodded. 'Anyway,' she said, rising, 'now that we've talked, perhaps we should be heading back to the house. I'll have to be up early tomorrow to catch my train.'

Nicholas stood up with her, his face in shadow.

'I don't want you to catch that train,' he said in a low voice.

A wave of confusion swept over her. Why was he doing this to her? Didn't he realise that those softly spoken words had the power to turn all her decisions on their head?

She gazed up at him mutely.

'You're so exquisite,' he muttered with a wrenched sigh. He reached out towards her with his hand, and Leigh's head snapped back.

'You mean you want to go to bed with me.'

'Of course I do, isn't it obvious? I've wanted to from the very first moment I saw you striding up that corridor at the magistrates' court, all that time ago. I took one look at you, and I don't think I've ever felt anything so powerful in my life before.'

'You don't mean that,' Leigh said helplessly. She sat back down, afraid that if she didn't her legs would collapse from underneath her. 'You thought I was a gold-digger, an opportunist. You said so!'

Her head was swimming and a thousand thoughts were jumbled chaotically in her mind, desperately trying to make sense out of what she was feeling.

'I was wrong. I never really believed that, but it helped for a while to believe the worst, since I could still pretend to myself that all I felt for you was some kind of primitive physical attraction.' He raked his fingers through his hair and his eyes when they met hers were defensive and sheepish at the same time. 'I didn't want you to get under my skin, dammit. I'd had a couple of near-misses with women who saw me as a meal ticket.'

'The girl at university?'

Nicholas looked at her in surprise. 'She was one of a few. But how the hell do you know? No, don't tell me, that conniving old grandfather of mine.'

She nodded.

'I might have guessed that he'd spare no effort in his little game of throwing us together.'

She shrugged. So what if he didn't think the worst of her? That didn't mean anything, did it? He still saw her as a desirable commodity, no strings attached. But a little flame of hope was licking into her reasoning.

'It didn't work though, did it?' she asked dully. 'I'm still not into sleeping with men just because they want me to.'

'Dammit, woman,' he said uncomfortably, 'listen to what I'm saying. It's not just that. Sleeping together. You . . . you do things to me, things I can't even find the words to explain, and I'm normally so clever with words.' She could hear the frustrated bewilderment in his voice, and trembled. 'I want you, Leigh. Right now. Here, if it were possible, but, as it's not, upstairs, in the decorum of a bedroom.' There was an urgency to him, and a soft groan escaped her lips.

'No,' she repeated weakly, 'I told you. Why don't you listen to me? I'm not a plaything. I don't operate with the same set of rules as you do.'

He didn't reply. He held out his hand, and this time she took it and felt an intense passion sweep over her, an electric current that held her in its grip.

She heard him book the room, the best in the hotel, took the lift up with him, all in silence, all with the sensation of events happening in a daze. It was what she had fought against so desperately. But she just couldn't fight any longer. Now she knew that she had to sleep with him, whatever the consequences.

She would be hurt, that was as inevitable as the rising and setting of the sun. But the pain would be less than the agony of a lifetime of regret, of knowing that she had sacrificed the only fulfilment she could ever have with a man to a set of rules. A set of rules which were relevant in the Victorian era, but were way out of date in the twentieth century.

The hotel room was massive. Her experience of hotel rooms was precisely nil, but, even so, she instinctively knew that this was luxury at its most unconstrained. Huge bed, beautiful wooden furniture, thick dusk-rose carpet that made her want to slip off her shoes and wriggle her toes in it.

'Your face can be so expressive,' Nicholas said with a laugh, although underneath she could sense that he was almost as tense as she was. Funny, when his experience of women was so wide.

'Meaning?' She threw him a teasing look, delighted by the fiery response it sparked off.

'You're a witch, woman,' he grated out, lifting her off her feet and dumping her unceremoniously on the bed. Then they were both laughing. He began to remove his clothing, staring down at her, willing her to look at him.

She did. Her eyes feasted on his deliberately slow movements. God, she wasn't laughing now. Her heart was beating so loudly that it drowned all the other little noises in the room, and a fine perspiration had broken out over her body.

Nicholas was marvellously unselfconscious about his body. He had rushed back to London straight from work, and was still in his suit. He tugged away the tie and unbuttoned the sober white shirt, exposing enough of his tanned, lean torso to make her feel heady. The man certainly knew the business of seduction, she thought.

There was something terribly intimate about undressing in front of a spectator. Nicholas watched her face as he stripped off, smiling slightly at her expression, then he sank on to the bed next to her and reached across, nuzzling her shoulder.

'Don't be afraid,' he murmured, his teeth gently nipping her skin, 'I won't hurt you.'

Leigh winced and closed her eyes. A physical blow would not have been more painful, because she knew how far from the truth he was. He could do more than hurt her—he could shatter her life into a million useless fragments. In fact, hadn't he already done as much? The person lying here in the bed bore only a physical resemblance to the one who had reluctantly travelled down to London with her brother.

'Leigh,' he murmured, 'sweet fool. It's that set of rules of yours, isn't it?'

She nodded and said, 'You're right. I am a fool.'

'Shall I tell you what my set of rules has always been?'

No, she wanted to shout, but she kept still, waiting for the inevitability of his answer.

'I've always put my career before everything else. Sure I've been out with women, lots of them, but I never let them intrude on what I felt was the most important part of my life—namely, legal success.'

The words sounded excruciatingly familiar. She could have quoted them word for word, if he had asked her.

'Until you came along, that is,' he muttered against her skin, and she felt a wave of pleasure wash over her.

'Pardon?'

'You heard, dammit!'

'I want to hear again.'

'You managed to throw me wildly off course.'

What he was saying was managing to throw her wildly off course. Leigh lay back, her eyes half closed as he slowly unbuttoned the front of her dress and slipped his hand underneath to caress her bare breast. She moaned and his fingers curved around the hardened nipple, rolling it between his fingers, then his mouth replaced his fingers and pulled wetly against it, sending fierce sensation shooting through her.

He tugged off her dress, tossing it on the ground, and buried his head between her breasts, his hands massaging them until she wanted to scream out for more. When he raised his head to look at her, his eyes were hot with passion.

'What are you trying to tell me, Nicholas?' Leigh dared to ask. After all, what had she got to lose? If he shot her a blank look, then she would be no worse off than she was half an hour ago when she decided to sleep with him, whatever the consequences. But maybe, just maybe, he would say that he cared for her, that she was more than simply a passing fancy. If he did, then her euphoria would last a lifetime. It would have to.

'What would you like me to say? That I love you?'

'Yes, please,' Leigh said in a tiny voice, closing her eyes and risking all, 'because I happen to love you, and, believe me, you weren't part of my plans either.'

'My darling.' He tilted her head back, and besieged her neck with kisses until she squirmed helplessly against him. 'Haven't you guessed by now? I thought I was so transparent! Like one of those lovesick adolescents I always pitied. I love you, you witch. I love you, and need you and want you. Just when I thought that life had no surprises left to offer, I met you, and now that I've got you in my arms I'm never going to let you go...'

Later, as they lay in each other's arms, his hand gently caressing the swell of her breast, Nicholas said thoughtfully, 'I wouldn't be a bit surprised if that crafty old devil hadn't had this in mind when he asked me to go up to Yorkshire and bail your brother out. And when he suggested that the best thing might have been if the two of you came down to London.'

'Do we forgive him?' Leigh teased, melting as his fingers found her hardened nipple.

'Difficult not to when we're walking up the aisle.'

Her eyes shone. 'Are you sure it's what you want?'

'Just try and talk me out of it,' he said roughly. 'And after that, how do you feel about living in London? With frequent visiting rights to Freddie and Grandfather?'

'Just try and talk me out of it,' she sighed happily. 'And how do you feel about a family? Because we haven't taken any precautions, and who knows where this lovemaking has led——?'

He stroked her stomach lovingly. 'What better place for all this sweet love to go,' he whispered with a smile, 'than to our baby?'

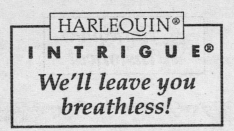

HARLEQUIN®

I N T R I G U E®

We'll leave you breathless!

If you've been looking for thrilling tales of
contemporary passion and sensuous love stories
with taut, edge-of-the-seat suspense—
then you'll *love* **Harlequin Intrigue!**

Every month, you'll meet four new heroes
who are guaranteed to make your spine tingle
and your pulse pound. With them you'll enter
into the exciting world of Harlequin Intrigue—
where your life is on the line
and so is your heart!

THAT'S INTRIGUE—DYNAMIC ROMANCE AT ITS BEST!

 HARLEQUIN®

I N T R I G U E®

Harlequin® Historical

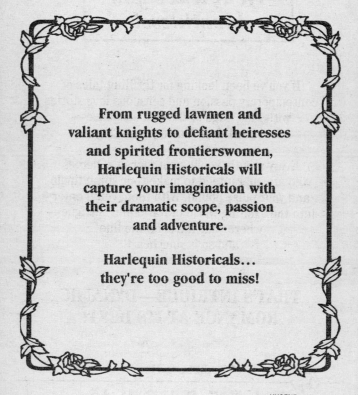

From rugged lawmen and
valiant knights to defiant heiresses
and spirited frontierswomen,
Harlequin Historicals will
capture your imagination with
their dramatic scope, passion
and adventure.

Harlequin Historicals...
they're too good to miss!

LOOK FOR OUR FOUR FABULOUS MEN!

Each month some of today's bestselling authors bring
four new fabulous men to Harlequin American Romance.
Whether they're rebel ranchers, millionaire power brokers
or sexy single dads, they're all gallant princes—and
they're all ready to sweep you into lighthearted fantasies
and contemporary fairy tales where anything is possible
and where all your dreams come true!

You don't even have to make a wish...
Harlequin American Romance will grant your every desire!

Look for Harlequin American Romance
wherever Harlequin books are sold!

HARLEQUIN SUPERROMANCE®

...there's more to the story!

Superromance. A *big* satisfying read about
unforgettable characters. Each month we offer
four very different stories that range from family
drama to adventure and mystery, from highly
emotional stories to romantic comedies—and
much more! Stories about people you'll
believe in and care about. Stories too
compelling to put down....

Our authors are among today's *best* romance
writers. You'll find familiar names and
talented newcomers. Many of them are
award winners—and you'll see why!

If you want the biggest and best
in romance fiction, you'll get it
from Superromance!

Available wherever Harlequin books are sold.

Not The Same Old Story!

Exciting, glamorous romance stories that take readers around the world.

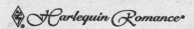

Sparkling, fresh and tender love stories that bring you pure romance.

Bold and adventurous—Temptation is strong women, bad boys, great sex!

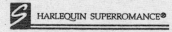

Provocative and realistic stories that celebrate life and love.

Contemporary fairy tales—where anything is possible and where dreams come true.

Heart-stopping, suspenseful adventures that combine the best of romance and mystery.

LOVE & LAUGHTER™

Humorous and romantic stories that capture the lighter side of love.

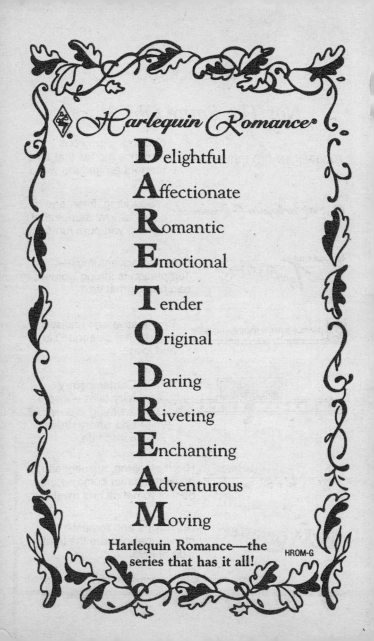

Harlequin Romance®

Delightful

Affectionate

Romantic

Emotional

Tender

Original

Daring

Riveting

Enchanting

Adventurous

Moving

Harlequin Romance—the
series that has it all!

HROM-G